M. G. LEONARD & SAM SEDGMAN

THE ARCTIC RAILWAY ASSASSIN

Illustrated by Elisa Paganelli

MACMILLAN CHILDREN'S BOOKS

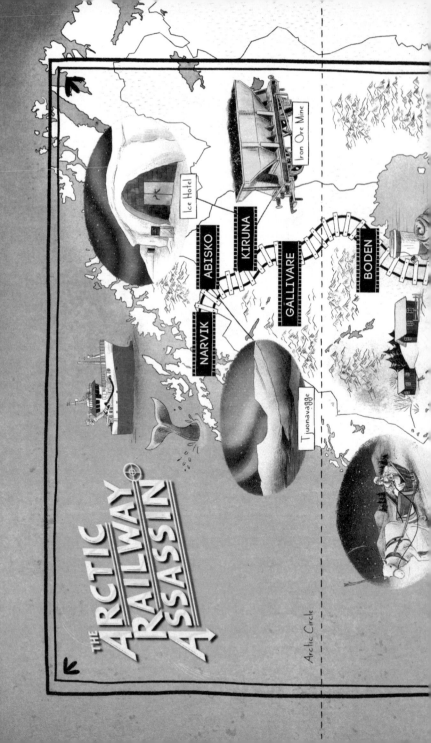

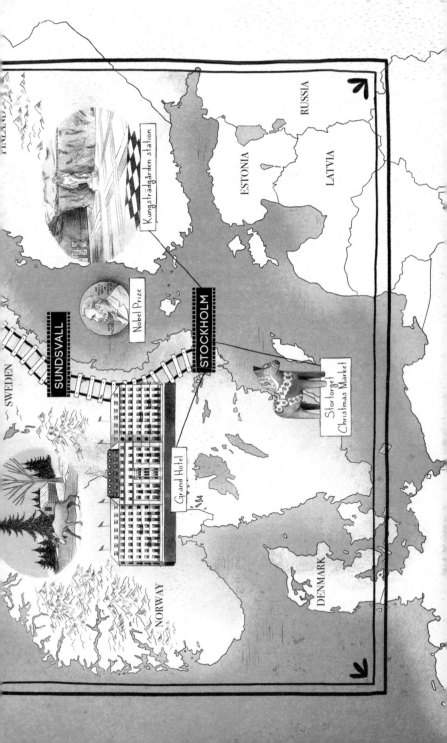

For Sarah Hughes,
our editor, who has kept us on track, with love.

'If I were not a physicist, I would probably be a musician.
I often think in music.'

Albert Einstein

CHAPTER ONE

UP IN THE AIR

Since he'd boarded the plane, Hal had covered three pages in his new sketchbook with portraits and doodles. Drawing helped him think clearly. It was the way he worked through puzzles and solved crimes. Turning to a fresh page, his practised hand conjured the aeroplane aisle onto the paper. His art pen swiftly drew the seats ahead of him and blank profiles for passengers' faces. *I'm making a mountain out of a molehill*, he thought to himself. *It could mean nothing.* He glanced up at the overhead locker where his rucksack was stowed.

On the way to Manchester airport, his mum had received a message from his uncle, asking Hal to bring Yorkshire Gold tea bags to Stockholm. They'd stopped at a supermarket. The box of tea was in his bag.

Why does Uncle Nat want Yorkshire Gold tea bags? The question was worrying Hal.

He drew the features of the man sitting in front of him, a short beard, moustache . . .

1

Hal was about to draw the baseball cap, which was flattening the man's fringe into a straight line above his thick eyebrows, when the passenger took it off. Hal lifted his pen, mildly annoyed that his subject had moved.

The tea bags were an ominous sign. When Hal had travelled across America on the California Comet, Uncle Nat had told him that if he was homesick or upset, he'd have a cup of Yorkshire Gold to make himself feel better. But Uncle Nat couldn't be homesick. He'd only been in Stockholm for three or four days. So, something must have upset him, Hal reasoned. He hoped it wasn't serious. He'd been looking forward to this trip all term. He didn't want anything to ruin it.

The man Hal was drawing leaned forward, pulling headphones from his bag. Hal saw the top of his outer ear was strangely flat. A female passenger was chatting away to him. Hal guessed the man found this annoying because she was still talking when he put the headphones on. She stopped abruptly and scowled. Hal caught her bitter expression with his pen and smiled to himself as he looked down at his drawing. He'd got it just right. The man leaned back and closed his eyes.

'Harrison?'

Hal looked up at the much-too-cheerful face of the flight attendant who'd been appointed his chaperone. He was a gangly young man whose constant smile and blue-checked jacket made him look like an entertainer at a holiday camp.

'We're going to start our descent into Stockholm soon,' he said. 'If you want to go to the toilet, this is your last chance

2

before the lights go on.' He tapped the seatbelt sign above Hal's head.

'I'm fine, thanks.'

Hal had been excited to fly to Sweden on his own, until he'd discovered that anyone under the age of fourteen had to be chaperoned by an air steward. Hal had protested that he was thirteen, well-travelled, and didn't need looking after, but apparently it was the rule. The flight attendant was kind but talked to him as if he were very young, and Hal found it annoying.

That was one of the things that made Nathaniel Bradshaw Hal's favourite uncle. He talked to Hal like he was a person,

not a child. Uncle Nat was a travel writer, and Hal had accompanied him on some amazing railway journeys. This trip, a long weekend away, was a Christmas present. His uncle was already in Stockholm. He'd been attending the Nobel Prize awards as a guest of an old friend. Hal was meeting him in the Swedish capital, and from there they were taking a sleeper train north, into the Arctic Circle, to a village called Abisko and a place called the Aurora Sky Station, to see the Northern Lights. Hal's heart skipped around his chest every time he thought about it. He'd already drawn a map of their route in the front of his sketchbook.

On the tray-table, beside his drawing, was a tin containing twelve squares of coloured paint and a small silver brush. He slid out the brush from its groove, dipped it into the plastic cup of water he'd got from the air steward, mixed a wash of blue in the lid and added colour to the man's denim jacket.

Uncle Nat had warned him he wouldn't be able to draw by daylight when they reached Abisko. The sun set in the Arctic Circle on the tenth of December and wouldn't rise again until January the fourth. Uncle Nat had called it the polar night. And so Hal had thought carefully about which art materials to bring on the trip. In the end, he'd chosen a set of four art pens, to draw the monochrome landscapes, the snow and the mountains, and his tin of watercolours for the Aurora Borealis. Uncle Nat had told him the Northern Lights lit up the skies with fluctuating waves of coloured light. He was going to try and capture the phenomenon with washes of paint.

'Ladies and gentlemen, we are about to begin our descent

4

into Stockholm. Please make sure your seatbelts are fastened, your baggage is stowed, and that your seats and tray-tables are in the upright position.'

Hal put away his paints, pens and sketchbook, handed the water to the air steward, then fastened his seatbelt.

As the plane dipped its wing, he looked out of the window at the advancing archipelago, stepping stones to the city of Stockholm, glittering like a tangle of Christmas lights on the edge of the Baltic Sea. He smiled. It felt good knowing that his uncle was down there, waiting to meet him in the airport. Whatever had upset Uncle Nat, Hal was certain that with his help, a magical train journey to the Arctic and a comforting cup of tea, everything would be all right.

CHAPTER TWO

THE ARLANDA EXPRESS

With his rucksack on his back, Hal followed the flight attendant through airport security, the baggage collection area, past a seven-foot Christmas tree dressed in white lights and giant gold baubles, and through the arrivals gate.

'There he is,' Hal said, immediately spotting his uncle at the front of the waiting crowd, dressed in a dinner jacket and bow tie. He waved.

'Mr Bradshaw?' the attendant asked as Uncle Nat came forward and hugged Hal. 'Can I see some identification please?'

'Of course.' Uncle Nat withdrew his passport from his inside jacket pocket and Hal saw a flash of turquoise silk lining. 'Good flight?' he asked Hal, as the attendant checked his photograph. 'I hope you're not too tired. I would have suggested an earlier plane, but the banquet only finished an hour ago.'

'I'm wide awake,' Hal assured him. He didn't mind staying up late one bit.

The flight attendant returned Uncle Nat's passport with a nod. 'I hope you enjoyed flying with us, Harrison,' he said, producing a lollipop from his pocket and handing it to Hal with a professional smile. 'We hope to see you again soon.'

'Um, yes. Thank you,' Hal replied, glancing at Uncle Nat, who suppressed a chuckle as the flight attendant walked away.

'The airport shuttle is this way,' Uncle Nat signalled.

'Mum got your message,' Hal said, dropping the lollipop into the nearest bin. 'About the Yorkshire Gold.' He studied his uncle's face. 'We stopped on the way to the airport, specially. I've got it in my bag.'

'That was very kind of you,' Uncle Nat replied. His face was unreadable. Hal watched him closely as they passed shuttered kiosks and illuminated adverts with Swedish slogans on their way to a bank of lifts. Uncle Nat tapped the call button. 'I could really do with a nice cup of tea when we get to the hotel.'

Stepping inside, Hal felt a sudden lightness as the lift descended quickly. When the doors pinged open, they exited onto an underground railway platform. Hal was amazed to see the dark station was hewn into the rock like a cave.

'How's your mum?' Uncle Nat asked, pausing to purchase Hal a train ticket from a banana-yellow machine.

'Oh, you know,' Hal replied. 'Rushing about getting everything ready for Christmas. Panicking about me going on an adventure with you in case something terrible happens.'

'Nothing terrible is going to happen.' Uncle Nat laughed.

'That's what I said.'

'And this year you're all coming to mine and James's for Christmas Day. We are cooking.' Uncle Nat peered over the rim of his tortoiseshell glasses as he held out Hal's ticket. 'What does that sister of mine have to get ready?'

'I don't know.' Hal shrugged. 'She's made an enormous Christmas pudding, and everyone is getting homemade jam and tomato chutney as a present, whether they like it or not. The kitchen's been off limits for weeks.'

'Sounds like escaping to the Arctic for a few days is exactly what you need.'

'Yes.' Hal beamed. 'I can't wait to board the night train to Narvik tomorrow.'

'I'll give you a whistle-stop tour of Stockholm in the morning,' Uncle Nat said, moving down the platform, coming to a standstill beneath a huge circular spotlight. 'Oh and, I hope you won't mind, but my friend Morti is travelling on the Narvik train with us as far as Kiruna.'

'Oh!' Hal tried to hide his disappointment. He'd been looking forward to spending time alone with his uncle.

'It's just for the first night. She has her own compartment, of course. We'll probably only see her at dinner.' He looked apologetic. 'She's letting us stay the night at her cabin in Kiruna on our way home.'

'She's going to be in Kiruna with us?'

'She wasn't going to be, but her plans have changed. Oh Hal, I can see you're disappointed. I'm sorry. I can't imagine Morti will want to do anything more than eat dinner with us and sleep on the train. She's had quite a week.'

And there it was: the facial expression that Hal had been watching for. Three horizontal lines in the centre of his uncle's forehead, created as both eyebrows stooped to meet in concern. There *was* something wrong and it had

9

something to do with his friend, Morti.

'Why's Morti had quite a week?' Hal asked, keeping his voice light.

'Mortimer Sorenson won the Nobel Prize for medicine this evening,' Uncle Nat replied. 'She's the one who invited me to Stockholm, to accompany her to the banquet. I thought you knew that?'

'Mum said your friend had won a Nobel Prize, but I didn't know their name.' Hal felt his neck getting hot. 'I've heard of the Nobel Prize, but I don't really know what it is,' he admitted.

'Let's just say, it's a big deal.' Uncle Nat smiled. 'It's the biggest prize of its kind in the world.'

The rails began to hum, and a white train with *Arlanda Express* in black along its side eased into the platform.

'This is us,' Uncle Nat said, climbing aboard as the doors slid open. 'The Arlanda Express travels at a hundred and sixty kilometres an hour, taking only eighteen minutes to reach Stockholm Central Station.' Hal followed his uncle into a spacious carriage and saw wide, brown upholstered seats with wooden arms. A handful of passengers boarded behind them, and Uncle Nat beckoned Hal down the aisle towards the connecting door and an empty carriage. 'It will only take us ten minutes to get from the station to the hotel, once we're in Stockholm. With any luck we'll be there before midnight.' He sat down.

Hal removed his rucksack, dropping into the seat beside his uncle. The doors hissed shut, and the Arlanda Express accelerated into the tunnel.

'What did your friend win the Nobel Prize for?' Hal asked.

'Mortimer is a specialist in ultrasound, a sonic scientist,' Uncle Nat replied in a quiet voice. 'She has discovered a way to disperse tumours in the body using sound waves.'

'And you are worried about her because . . . ?' Hal let the question hang.

'I . . .' Uncle Nat frowned. 'Hang on, how do you know that I'm worried about her?'

'You must be worried about something. You asked me to bring you Yorkshire Gold tea,' Hal replied, giving him a knowing look.

'Yes, but . . .'

'Are you worried about Morti?' Hal persisted.

'Yes, I am,' Uncle Nat admitted. 'Very . . . but—'

'Why are you worried?'

'The Nobel Prize has shone a spotlight on Mortimer's work.' Uncle Nat sighed. 'Ever since it was announced in October, a series of inexplicable things have happened to her.' He paused. 'She asked me to accompany her to the awards banquet because she's scared.'

'Scared of what?'

'If only we knew.' Uncle Nat shook his head.

'How do you know her?'

'We met at Cambridge University. Mortimer was studying physics and medicine. We were both members of Footlights, a theatre club, and we've been friends ever since. Mortimer and I share a love of music.' Uncle Nat reached a finger into his collar, unfastening his bow tie.

'You said inexplicable things have been happening to her?' Hal leaned close. 'What kind of things?'

'Hal, it's late.' Uncle Nat looked away. 'I appreciate your concern, I really do. But I want our journey tomorrow to be the wondrous Christmas treat I intended. This time, I'm going to prove to your mother than we can take a train trip together without encountering crime.'

'I understand.' Hal nodded. 'Although, if we're travelling on the Narvik train together tomorrow, it's going to be hard not to ask her about it.'

Uncle Nat shook his head, a thin smile on his lips. 'You're incorrigible.'

'I like solving puzzles and mysteries. Is that so bad?' Hal asked. 'I might be able to help your friend if you tell me about it.'

'How about we let Mortimer decide?'

'Okay.' Hal grinned. 'I can't wait to meet her.'

'I left her in the hotel bar when I came to get you. She may still be there.'

Hal leaned back in his seat and found himself beaming at his own reflection in the dark window. He'd missed his uncle. When they were together exciting things always happened.

CHAPTER THREE

THE SONIC SCIENTIST

To Hal's delight, fat flakes of snow were drifting lazily from the night sky when they came out of Stockholm Central Station. He stuck out his tongue and caught one. Despite it being nearly midnight, they were able to hop on a tram. The streets were almost empty. Reflected streetlights twinkled in the dark waterways and Hal marvelled at the bridges that united the built-up islands, making a city.

The tram dropped them outside the Grand Hotel. Uncle Nat swept Hal through the giant revolving doors and they emerged in a marble-floored lobby.

'Would you like to see if Morti is still in the bar?' Uncle Nat asked. 'If you're tired, you can always meet her at breakfast?'

'I'm not tired,' Hal replied, which wasn't true, but he'd caught the scent of a mystery and he wanted to see where it led.

They climbed some stairs and Hal followed his uncle into a bar.

Sitting in the far corner at a baby grand piano was a

woman dressed in a dinner suit like Uncle Nat's. Her white bow tie and the top button of her shirt were undone, and she wore a chunky green necklace of hexagons. Her grey hair was cropped very short at the sides and slicked up at the front to make a tall quiff. Her eyes were closed as she played. There was an empty glass sitting on a coaster on the top of the piano.

'Morti, I'm back,' Uncle Nat said, making a beeline for her.

Her eyelids lifted. Intelligent hazel eyes brushed over Uncle Nat and settled on Hal.

'Hello. You must be Harrison.' She smiled warmly, reaching out a hand decorated with chunky silver rings. 'I am an old friend of your uncle's. Mortimer Sorenson. You should call me Morti, all my friends do.'

'My friends call me Hal,' he replied, shaking her hand.

'Nathaniel tells me you are a talented artist.'

Hal flushed with pleasure.

'Excuse me.' A woman with a dark fringe and ponytail and carrying a circular tray approached them. 'Can I get you something to drink? The bar will be closing soon.'

'Just water, I think,' said Uncle Nat. 'We won't be staying long.'

The waitress nodded, leaning past him to pick up the empty glass from the piano, and moved away.

'Shall we sit?' Morti rose from the piano, draping her suit jacket over the back of an adjacent chair. Uncle Nat mirrored her, hanging his jacket on the back of another chair as he sat down beside her. Hal took the opposite seat, blinking his eyes to wake himself up. The dim lighting in the warm bar was making him feel sleepy.

'Did Uncle Nat tell you that I like to solve mysteries as well as draw?' Hal asked Morti.

'Do you know, he didn't.' Morti smiled at Uncle Nat. 'But I've read about a few of your cases in the newspapers. It seems you two are a lot alike.'

'We are.' Hal felt a little put out that his uncle hadn't mentioned his detective skills to his friend. 'When I arrived, I could see he was worrying about the inexplicable things that've been happening to you. I wondered if I could help?'

'I'm not sure if you can.' Morti shook her head. 'The police haven't been able to make sense of it.'

'Let me try.'

'All right then, well, this will sound peculiar,' Morti said, folding her hands into her lap, 'but my possessions keep disappearing.'

'Which possessions?'

'Let me start at the beginning. The first odd thing happened nearly two months ago. My apartment in Copenhagen was burgled.'

'Oh!' Hal exclaimed. 'That's awful.'

'It was an unpleasant experience.' Mortimer nodded. 'The place was turned upside down: my papers scattered, my drawers pulled out, my clothes on the floor, but the thieves must've been startled because nothing was taken.'

'Nothing at all?'

'I went through everything carefully. Nothing was gone.' She sighed. 'The police found no fingerprints. Nobody witnessed anybody coming in or out of my apartment. There was nothing more anyone could do.'

'You live on your own?' Hal asked.

A troubled expression passed over Mortimer's face. 'I do now.'

Hal glanced at Uncle Nat.

'You should tell him everything, Morti,' Uncle Nat said softly.

Mortimer reached out and struck a series of keys on the piano. 'What do you know about the science of sound, Hal?'

'I know sound is made of waves,' Hal replied, 'although I don't really know what that means. Uncle Nat told me you're a sonic scientist.'

'A sonic scientist?' She smiled at Nat, then turned back to Hal. 'Sound is a vibration that moves invisible particles in the air. We call this movement a wave. Bats navigate in the dark using sonic waves. That's how humans came to invent sonar, by learning from bats and how they use sound to see. Now we use ultrasound imaging to see things inside the human body. The first scan pictures of a baby are usually done using ultrasound. Sound waves can pass through fluid but reflect when they hit a solid surface. Multiple frequencies are used to create an image.'

Hal thought back to the strange grey-and-white picture that his mum had brought home from the hospital when she'd been pregnant with his little sister Ellie. It had looked like a white blob surrounded by weird grey shapes. It took him a while to see the baby. He hadn't realized the picture had been taken using sound.

'Have you ever heard of someone being able to smash a glass by singing?' Mortimer asked.

Hal nodded. 'Opera singers can do it.'

'Ha! Well, no, it's not exclusive to opera singers, but it is possible. If you tap a glass, you will hear a ringing noise;

that is the frequency of the glass. If you can sing at the same frequency, loud enough and long enough, the glass will smash. It's called a destructive resonant frequency.'

'What does frequency mean? Is it the note? Like a middle C on a piano?'

'Frequency is the rate per second of the vibration. The higher the frequency, the higher in pitch the sound. Middle C on a piano is –' reaching out again, she played the note – '261.63 vibrations per second. That's how *frequent* the vibrations are.'

'Objects like a glass have a frequency?'

'All things have a natural frequency, or a set of frequencies, at which they vibrate.'

Hal's mind reeled at this midnight physics lesson. 'But what's this got to do with your flat being burgled?'

'I'm getting to that. My work, for which I was awarded the Nobel Prize this evening, was for finding what has been called the *magic frequency*: the destructive resonant frequency that can shatter cancer cells.'

'You can cure cancer with sound?' Hal's mouth dropped open.

'Not yet, but at some point in the future . . .' Morti nodded. 'I hope so.'

'You definitely deserve a prize for that! That's amazing!'

'It has taken years, searching for the magic frequency. We tried thousands of different combinations.' She played three notes on the piano, a chord. 'But I wasn't on this quest alone. My husband, Björn, worked with me.'

'Did he get the Nobel Prize too?' Hal frowned, wondering

why Mortimer had taken Uncle Nat to the awards and not her husband.

'No. Björn is in prison,' Mortimer said flatly. 'Before I discovered the magic frequency, I discovered that my husband was collecting data on other frequencies. Resonant frequencies with dangerously destructive powers.'

'Dangerous?'

'If we can shatter cancer cells, Harrison, we can shatter other types of cells inside a human.' She dropped her head, closing her eyes as she drew in a long breath. 'Björn was collecting frequencies that, when used together, would kill a person instantly.'

'Oh!' Hal was shocked.

'When I realized this, I confronted Björn. He admitted to trying to create what he called a Kill Code. A pattern of frequencies that could be channelled through a sonic weapon and sold to the highest bidder.'

'What did you do?' Hal was suddenly hanging on Morti's every word.

'I could see that Björn's mind had been infected with greed. I pretended to be excited by the money such a weapon might bring us. Then, once he was asleep, I called a good friend.' She smiled at Uncle Nat. 'He had a contact in the Danish government. Secret service officers came in the night and arrested Björn.' She wrung her hands. 'We'd only been married a month.' She gave her head a little shake. 'I immediately went to our laboratory and destroyed my husband's work. Every scrap of research he'd ever created, I deleted or burned. I wiped the hard drive of his computer.'

'How long ago was this?' Hal could see that Mortimer was still upset by what had happened.

'Nearly two years.'

'Have you seen Björn since that night?'

'No. I don't want to.'

'Do you think the burglary has something to do with him?'

'How can it be? He's in a high-security prison.' Her eyes dipped as she thought about him, but then she took a breath and looked up. 'The burglary is only the first in a series of strange incidents. A week or so later, I started to feel like I was being watched when I walked to work. I changed my route several times, I'd turn suddenly, slip down alleyways. I never saw anyone, but I'm certain somebody was following me.' She curled her fingers into a fist, which she held to her chest. 'I felt it here.' She looked at Hal intensely, as if daring him not to believe her. 'In my laboratory, at the end of the day, I always lock the window and the door before I leave. But every morning, the window is unlocked. How can this be?' She paused, but not long enough for Hal to make a suggestion. 'Nothing is ever out of place. But I knew someone was coming in at night and monitoring my work. So I set up a camera, directed it at the window.' She rubbed the back of her neck with her hand. 'It shows nothing. Nothing comes near the window. And yet in the morning it is unlocked.'

'That's creepy,' Hal glanced at Uncle Nat.

'Sometimes, when I'm with a friend at a bar or restaurant, and I look in my handbag, all my possessions are tumbled around, as if someone's been through my bag when I wasn't looking.' Mortimer let out a heavy sigh of frustration. 'And when I arrived in Stockholm airport on Monday, my suitcase came off the baggage conveyor looking like it had been slashed with a knife!'

'Do you think someone is looking for the Kill Code?'

'That is what I thought at first, but why would they follow me to Stockholm? I don't have it. As far as I know, Björn didn't complete his project. And I have systematically destroyed everything of his both in the lab and at home. There is no Kill Code.'

'You're sure?' Uncle Nat asked.

'Positive.'

The clock behind the bar struck one.

'It's late.' Uncle Nat looked at Hal. 'Bedtime.'

'I'll think about everything you've told me,' Hal said on the way through reception.

'Thank you, Hal. I appreciate your help.'

They bid Mortimer goodnight as she got out of the lift, arranging to meet her at breakfast, then carried on up to their floor.

'That's strange.' Uncle Nat patted his pockets as they stood outside the door to their room. 'I could've sworn my phone and room key were in this jacket pocket.' He paused, trying to remember the last time he had them. 'Oh blast! I've been all over the city this evening. They could be anywhere!' He scratched his head. 'Hal, I'm going to have to go down to reception, see if anyone's handed them in, and get a spare key.'

'I'll wait here,' Hal said, but as the lift doors opened, he heard a noise inside their hotel room. The hairs on the back of his neck rose. 'Wait,' he called out, hurrying after his uncle, 'on second thought, I'll come with you.'

CHAPTER FOUR

THE CHRISTMAS MARKET

When he woke up, Hal stretched, inhaling the smell of fresh cotton sheets, and sat bolt upright as he remembered where he was. Today he would board the night train to Narvik with Uncle Nat and Morti, to travel to the Arctic. Hal had questions he wanted to ask Morti over breakfast. He was excited about investigating the mysterious things she'd described last night, and a little annoyed that he'd let his imagination get the better of him when Uncle Nat lost his key. The hotel room had been empty when they'd finally got inside, and his uncle was certain nothing had been touched. Hal sighed happily as he looked around the grand room; the adventure had begun.

Leaping out of bed, Hal drew back the curtains and saw that an icy mist had settled over Stockholm. He listened at the adjoining door connecting his room to Uncle Nat's but heard nothing. Carefully, he opened it an inch.

'Ah, you're up.' Uncle Nat was sitting at a desk in the window, writing in his journal. 'I wasn't sure how long to leave you. It was a late night last night.'

'Have I missed breakfast?' Hal asked, seeing his uncle's bag was on the bed, already packed.

'No.' He looked at his left wrist, where he wore three watches. 'In fact, if you throw some clothes on, we'll be in time to meet Morti.'

Hal scrambled out of his pyjamas, got dressed and followed his uncle out of the room.

Breakfast was served in the hotel restaurant. Hal ate a bowl of muesli with berries and yogurt, while watching Uncle Nat eat crispbread he called knäckebröd, covered in slices of cheese and red peppers, and a hard-boiled egg with a fish roe-paste garnish. Hal thought it was an unusual breakfast.

'Mr Bradshaw?' A porter from the reception desk approached their table.

'That's me.' Uncle Nat wiped his mouth with the linen napkin.

'Ms Sorenson left this with reception, early this morning. She asked that we made sure you got it before you left.' He handed Uncle Nat an envelope.

'I don't suppose anyone has handed in my phone this morning?'

'I'm afraid not, sir.'

'And did you manage to get through to City Hall?'

'We've left a message about your missing phone.'

Uncle Nat thanked the porter and turned to Hal. 'I was wondering where Morti had got to.' He opened the envelope and tipped it upside down. A pair of keys on a ring with a fob dropped into his hand, accompanied by a hotel compliments slip. He read it aloud.

Dear Nat,

I'm sorry for my sudden disappearance. Something urgent has come up that means I can no longer travel with you to Kiruna.

Here are the keys to my cabin. Make yourself at home. I am hoping to be there when you return from the Aurora Sky Station. If for any reason we miss each other, please leave the keys at the reception of the Ice Hotel. They will look after them for me.

Thank you for coming to Stockholm, the awards ceremony and the banquet. It meant a great deal to have you there. You must also thank your nephew, Hal, for listening to my strange stories last night. It was good of him.

You are a true friend, and I hope I am yours.

Mortimer

Uncle Nat turned the slip of paper over, but the back was blank. He looked at Hal, and the three horizontal lines returned above his dipping eyebrows. 'How odd.' He turned the keys in the palm of his hand.

To his surprise, Hal found that he was disappointed Morti wouldn't be travelling with them. He had questions about her burglary, and he wanted to know more about the terrifying Kill Code. 'What's odd?'

'That something should come up so early in the morning. And why didn't Morti come to my room and give me the keys herself?'

'The note says it was urgent. Perhaps a relative is sick and she didn't want to wake us.'

'Maybe,' Uncle Nat conceded, putting the keys down on the table and picking up his coffee. His eyes glazed over as he fell to thinking.

Hal examined the key fob. It was a piece of folded leather with three golden rings. A large and medium-sized ring were attached to the end of the leather fob with two keys dangling from them – a bronze key with a circular barrel and fork-shaped end, the other a flat silver key with a jagged, zigzag edge. A small decorative gold ring hung flat against the folded leather fob. Pulling the folded leather apart, Hal searched for any hidden message or suspicious marks. But it looked like an ordinary well-worn leather key fob with a pair of door keys on it. Disappointed, he laid them on his opened sketchbook, picked out a pen, and drew a speedy study of them as he shovelled the rest of his muesli into his mouth.

With Morti went his hope of solving a crime on this trip. 'Do you think someone stole the room key from your jacket pocket to break into our hotel room? I did hear that noise last night,' Hal said, grasping at the last dangling thread of a mystery.

'No.' Uncle Nat smiled at Hal. 'My Mont Blanc pen was sitting on the desk in plain view of the door. If someone had gone into the room and had a root around, I would have noticed. Nothing was touched, moved or taken, and if anyone had broken in, they would have stolen my pen.'

'Your pen?' Hal scoffed.

'Yes. It's worth more than all of my six watches combined.' Uncle Nat chuckled at Hal's astonished expression.

'What? I didn't know pens could be that fancy. Well . . . perhaps the thief was after your mobile phone, then. You said it was in the same pocket.'

'Ha! That old thing?' Uncle Nat drained the last of his coffee. 'It barely connects to the internet. It's only good for calls and texts. You couldn't give it away. It's about time I got a new one.' He sighed. 'No, I'm afraid something horribly dull happened to my phone and the room key. You see, Mortimer and I were at a banquet last night, and there was dancing. I fear I may have lost my phone and the key while doing the funky chicken.'

'Oh!' Hal couldn't disguise his horror at the idea of his

uncle dancing, and Uncle Nat laughed.

'We should get a move on. Stockholm is a beautiful city and I wanted to take you for a wander around the Christmas market in Stortorget. I need to get a gift for James.'

'I could get something for Mum.'

'Perhaps a Dala wooden horse? They're hand-carved and painted – a symbol of Sweden, and they're meant to bring good luck.'

'Mum likes horses. Will they have them at the market?'

'I believe so.' Uncle Nat picked up Morti's keys and her note, putting them into his inside jacket pocket, and got up. 'Our train isn't until five o'clock, so we've plenty of time to explore.'

Once they'd packed, they left their bags in a luggage room behind the hotel's reception desk, and travelled through the revolving doors out into Stockholm.

'The snow has settled,' Hal exclaimed with glee, looking down at his footprints.

'We're heading to that island opposite,' Uncle Nat said as he buttoned up his peacoat and tucked his cherry-red scarf inside the neck.

They crossed the bridge to Gamla Stan and entered a spider's web of medieval streets lined with little shops. As they made their way through the winding lanes, Hal enjoyed the festive windows. In one, toy penguins in Christmas hats were dancing before a fluffy polar bear sucking its thumb. *Fourteen days till Christmas*, Hal thought to himself and smiled. This was going to be the best Christmas ever.

The street widened into a cobbled market square, hemmed in by old buildings painted rust red and blushing orange. Shoppers bustled between rows of red-painted wood cabins with snow-covered roofs strung with evergreen garlands. A huge fir tree sprouted up on one side of the square, decked with lights and dusted with snow. The scents of cinnamon and chocolate tempted Hal forward.

'Lovely, isn't it?' Uncle Nat said with a happy sigh. 'You'd never guess this square was home to the 1520 Stockholm Bloodbath, when King Christian II killed all who opposed him.'

Hal snorted with surprise at this gruesome nugget of history and followed his uncle into the maze of stalls. They passed vendors selling porcelain holiday decorations, cured meats, candles, and homemade jams.

'Look at these!' Hal exclaimed, going to a cabin displaying beautifully painted wooden horses of all sizes. 'I think Mum would like a red one.' He picked up a wooden horse as big as his hand. 'She can put it on the mantelpiece in her Christmas display.'

While Uncle Nat paid for the horse, and the stall keeper wrapped it in a paper bag, Hal glanced at the next stall, where a woman in blue and red robes was selling carved jewellery made from reindeer antlers. A girl about Hal's age was sitting beside her, also dressed in a blue robe and a red hat. She was playing with the end of one of her long brown plaits and looking bored.

'There are reindeer in Sweden?' Hal asked his uncle.

'Oh yes,' said Uncle Nat, following Hal's gaze to the woman in traditional dress. 'The Sámi people are famous reindeer herders. They've lived in the north of Sweden, Norway, Finland and Russia for centuries. If we're lucky we may see reindeer in Kiruna.'

'Look at these.' Hal was drawn to a stall selling little wooden men in cheery red robes, only their bulbous noses visible between their curly beards and red hats.

'Tomte gnomes. They're supposed to look after your home.'

'Can we get one for Ellie?' Hal asked. 'They're cute.'

Uncle Nat found a brass nutcracker shaped like an alligator, which crunched chestnuts between its jaws. 'James will love this. He can roast the chestnuts on our hearth.'

Hal found himself staring at the Sámi girl on the next stall and wondering whether she was a reindeer herder. He thought it would be a brilliant thing to do. He made a note of her interesting dress, deciding to draw it later.

'I don't know about you, but I could do with a hot drink,' Uncle Nat said. 'There's a cafe serving drinks from a hatch over there.'

Hal saw two chalkboard menus on the wall either side of the window. One in Swedish, and one in English saying TAKEAWAY DRINKS – SANDWICHES – SWEETS.

'Does everyone in Sweden speak English?' Hal wondered as they joined the short queue for drinks.

'Not everyone, but most Swedes know a bit of English.'

Uncle Nat ordered a hot chocolate, a coffee and a couple of cinnamon buns. As he lifted the hot drinks from the waitress in the cafe hatch, a woman in a camel-coloured coat, wearing a leopard-print headscarf and oversized sunglasses, bumped into him. He jumped back to avoid spilling the drinks down his front.

'*Jag är ledsen,*' the woman said, while, quick as a flash, Hal saw her slip her hand into Uncle Nat's coat pocket and pull out his wallet.

'*Jag är ledsen!*' Hal yelled, not knowing what it meant, as he whacked the flat of his hand down onto the woman's arm. She dropped the wallet, glancing at Hal over her shoulder as she hurried away into the market.

'What on earth . . . ?' Uncle Nat exclaimed.

Hal bent down and picked up the wallet from the ground. Taking his hot chocolate, he handed it back to his uncle, noticing that the Sámi girl was watching him.

CHAPTER FIVE

KUNGSTRÄDGÅRDEN

'Are you all right?' Hal asked his uncle.

'Didn't spill a drop,' Uncle Nat reassured him, with a smile. 'Let's perch on those steps for a bit.' He nodded towards a building with an imposing facade: steps leading to a pair of glass doors with a giant gold medal emblazoned on them. On the medal was the profile of a man's head.

'That's the Nobel Prize Museum!' Hal exclaimed. 'Is that where you were last night?'

'No, the banquet is at the City Hall.' Uncle Nat brushed the snow off a step before sitting down. 'Well done on stopping that pickpocket.' He handed Hal a cinnamon bun. 'That was quick thinking. We would have been a bit stuck without my bank cards.' He looked out across the square and took a sip of coffee. 'I should've known touristy places like this are a magnet for pickpockets.'

'Oh wow!' Hal's eyes widened as he took a big bite. 'These are the softest, most delicious buns I've ever tasted.' It was gone in five mouthfuls. Dusting off his hands, Hal took a swig of his hot chocolate, then pulled out his sketchbook and pen while he still had an image of the pickpocket in his mind's eye.

Uncle Nat watched him call her likeness onto the page with only a few lines. 'You're getting really fast.'

'I've been practising.'

'What did you make of Morti's story last night?'

'I have questions,' Hal replied. 'I wanted to talk to her today about it, on the train.'

'What would you have asked her?'

'Well, according to her, after her husband was arrested, she went back to doing her research and everything was normal.'

'Yes. It was.'

'How long for?'

'Nearly two years.'

'And then two months ago she was burgled.'

'Yes.'

'So what happened two months ago to start the strange things happening?'

Uncle Nat blinked at this simple question. 'Well, I suppose that was when the winners of the Nobel Prize were announced. The ceremony comes two months later.'

'Then that announcement – or possibly something else – made someone start doing these things to Morti,' Hal reasoned. 'I think either someone is angry or jealous and wants to punish Morti for getting such a big prize, or . . . someone thinks she has the Kill Code and is looking for it.'

'But she doesn't.'

'Morti may think she's destroyed all her husband's work,

34

but what if she hasn't? Or she has, but someone thinks she hasn't.'

'Morti is thorough.' Uncle Nat shook his head. 'She told me that she'd put everything of Björn's into boxes and had it incinerated. She wiped the hard drive of his computer and then donated it to a local school. She moved out of their house into a small apartment and got a new laboratory. She's tried to have a completely fresh start. I don't see how she could have that Kill Code.'

'Then somebody is really jealous.' Hal looked down at the picture of the pickpocket in his sketchbook. 'You were with Morti at the Nobel ceremony. Perhaps that's made you a target.'

'I don't think so.' Uncle Nat waved this idea away with his hand. 'I'm glad we're getting on a train to the Arctic later this afternoon. We can leave all of this Kill Code business behind.'

'I wouldn't mind if there was a crime to solve on the train.' Hal finished his hot chocolate and smacked his lips. 'Being on a train and solving crimes with you is the best thing in the world.'

Uncle Nat smiled. 'I'm not sure your mum would agree.'

'Yeah, but she's not here, is she?' Hal pointed to the glass doors behind them. 'Can we go in the Nobel Prize Museum?'

'Yes, but we're not investigating anything.'

'Whatever you say,' Hal replied, getting to his feet and grinning.

Hanging from the ceiling of the main hall of the Nobel

Museum were posters of every previous Nobel Prize winner. Morti wasn't up there yet. Hal discovered that Alfred Nobel became rich when he invented dynamite, for use in mining. He was later criticized for making money from war, so he set up the Nobel Prize in 1901, giving all his money to fund awards in medicine, physics, chemistry, literature and peace.

Hal thought about dynamite. It was something that could be used for good, helping humans mine the earth for minerals, but it could also be used to hurt people, by blowing them up. It seemed to him that this dilemma mirrored what Morti had described with the sonic frequencies. Her magic frequency could be used to get rid of cancer, which was amazing, but the Kill Code, a sound that could kill someone, was terrifying.

They came to an exhibit all about the annual Nobel banquet that took place in Stockholm City Hall. 'It says here that the prizes are awarded to the new laureates by the Swedish king,' Hal read from a plaque. 'Did you meet the king last night before you came to the airport to get me?'

'Yes, Carl XVI and Queen Silvia,' Uncle Nat replied, 'but only for a minute.'

Hal glanced at his uncle, impressed.

'Look.' Uncle Nat pointed at a wall with a giant blown-up newspaper article on it. 'There's Morti.'

They read the article, which explained who the five winners were this year and why. Beside four other portraits was a picture of Morti. Hal studied it. She was wearing a serious expression, lab coat and looking every bit the scientist. A sombre polo neck and trousers, no chunky necklace of hexagons, but a simple chain with a ring suspended from it. It was the portrait of a Nobel Prize winner.

'We've a few hours before we have to be at the station for the night train,' Uncle Nat said, glancing at the three wrist watches on his left arm. 'There's so much I could show you in Stockholm, but I really want to take you on the metro.'

'The underground?' Hal was surprised.

'The Stockholm metro has been described as the world's longest art gallery. Most of the stations have installations, paintings or mosaics created by over a hundred artists, and they're wildly different from one another. Let's go back to the hotel and grab our bags, then we can hotfoot it over to Kungsträdgården, the King's Garden, and get the metro to Central Station. We'll pick up a sandwich and some fruit there, for lunch.'

They made their way through the winding streets of Gamla Stan and on to the Strömbron bridge. Hal glanced back at the island and thought he saw a figure dart into a doorway. He frowned, but said nothing to his uncle, who was talking about some king called Gustav III who'd been assassinated at a masked ball. He looked back several times, but saw nothing. Was his imagination playing tricks on him again? Thinking about the Kill Code must have unnerved him, because he felt as though they were being followed.

When they reached the hotel, Uncle Nat peered at him. 'Hal, are you all right?'

'Yes, just cold,' Hal reassured him.

'Let's get inside and warm up a bit while we get our bags.

It's only a ten-minute walk to the metro station and it won't be cold underground.'

When they emerged from the Grand Hotel with their bags, fresh flakes of snow tumbled from the battleship-grey sky.

Hal marvelled at the strangeness of the light. 'Is it getting dark already?'

'Yes. Unnerving, isn't it?' Uncle Nat said, obviously enjoying the strangeness. 'This way.' He strode off, and Hal followed him to Kungsträdgården park. He occasionally glanced about, or turned suddenly, but he didn't see anything or anyone suspicious.

The park was lit up by thousands of fairy-lights in chains from tree to twinkling tree. Towering reindeers made of lights guarded the four corners of a piazza, and in the middle of the park, smiling people whirled around a colourful ice rink. The smell of burnt sugar, the gaiety of the festive lights and the happy skaters whirled Hal's dark thoughts away.

'Over there.' Uncle Nat pointed at a signpost with a white lamp illuminating a bold blue T. 'That's the sign for the metro.'

They crossed a road with tram tracks and turned a corner to the entrance. Between the silver double doors stood a red stone statue of a bearded man dressed as a Viking or gladiator, Hal wasn't sure which.

Inside, escalators swept down into the floor and the low ceiling above them sloped at the same angle as the moving stairs. The station was quiet. Hal felt like he was descending into the bowels of the earth. 'This is a really long escalator.'

'Kungsträdgården is the deepest metro station in

Stockholm.' Uncle Nat said, stepping off and turning to see Hal's reaction to the incredible cavern painted with patchwork patterns of red, green and white.

'It's like a prehistoric cave!' Hal exclaimed.

'When they dug out the stations, they sprayed the rock face with concrete, instead of cladding it. That's what makes it feel like a cave.'

Hal rushed over to a barrier and looked down into an illuminated granite pit containing bits of columns and ornate stone cornices from buildings. 'What's this?' There were plants and moss growing between them, and to the side an iron lamp post. 'It looks like an archaeological dig.'

'These are relics collected when Stockholm was redeveloped,' Uncle Nat replied, coming to stand beside him. 'But the most interesting thing about this station is that scientists recently discovered it has a unique ecosystem.'

'Ecosystem?' Hal looked around.

'Yes. Living down here are crane flies, fungus, unusual types of moss and a rare cave dwarf spider that shouldn't be found in this part of the world. I read that the ecosystem thrives on the chalk that drips from the ceiling, the artificial light and the human detritus that we shed as we pass through it.'

'Detritus?' Hal asked, noticing tiny rivulets of water and green algae growing on the wall closest to him.

'Skin cells, hair, that kind of thing.'

Hal winced at this fact. It was gross.

They walked through the cavernous hall with its green ceiling until the way split left and right, leading to two train platforms. Standing at the intersection was a salmon-coloured statue of a naked man. Uncle Nat pointed to a blue train waiting for passengers. They stepped into a mustard-yellow carriage and sat down. They were the only people in it. Just as the doors were closing, a girl wearing a sandy-coloured beanie and thick scarf hurried on, walking past them to sit at the far end. She had headphones on and was bobbing her head to music.

As the train moved away into the tunnel, Hal pulled out his sketchbook and doodled a picture of the Kungsträdgården station. He had never imagined a metro station could be so weird and wonderful. As his pen marked the page, he felt like he was leaving the Kill Code mystery behind. Soon they would be at Central Station, and boarding a train to the Arctic.

CHAPTER SIX

DRAWING
INSTRUMENTS

Central metro station wasn't as magical as Kungsträd-gården, but it was fantastic. The cavernous walls and ceilings were painted in a floral pattern of blue and white. One day, Hal thought, he'd like to travel the full length of the metro and see every single station.

Rising on an escalator, they found themselves in the middle of a bustling shopping centre. Uncle Nat pointed to a supermarket. 'Let's get ourselves lunch and snacks for the journey.'

Hal chose a cheese roll, a bag of crisps, a bottle of water and two large bars of Plopp chocolate. He found the name funny and decided to give one to his dad for Christmas.

As soon as they were out of the supermarket, Hal ate his roll. Walking around a city made you hungry.

'We're early,' said Uncle Nat. 'But usually you can board a sleeper train a while before departure. Shall we find out?'

Hal nodded eagerly. He couldn't wait to explore their compartment, get cosy, and set out on their adventure to the Arctic.

The entrance to the overground station was at the other end of the shopping centre. The waiting hall had a high, arched ceiling, with a bank of departure screens. Hal and Uncle Nat examined them before marching happily through the ticket barriers towards platform twelve, which turned out to be a stark, plain concrete strip.

'What time is it?' Hal asked as they walked along the platform.

'Two fifty-five.'

'It's dark.' Hal looked up at the sky, feeling disoriented. 'It could be nine o'clock at night.'

'Stockholm only gets an hour of full sunlight a day in December,' Uncle Nat told him. 'When we arrive in Abisko, we'll be above the Arctic Circle. There'll be no sunlight at all.'

'It's dark all day?'

'Reflected light, off snow, creates an otherworldly light that you wouldn't call daylight, but you can see by it.' Uncle Nat was looking up and down the empty platform. 'There's no sign of our train. Let's ask the station guard when it will arrive.'

Looking across at the row of stark platforms opposite, all under corrugated iron roofs, where people were waiting or boarding trains, Hal spotted the girl from the metro, with her sandy beanie and headphones. She seemed to feel his gaze and looked up. He caught her eye and smiled, but she looked away and a train pulled into her platform – dove grey with silver carriages. There was a functional, bold feel to the design of Swedish rolling stock that Hal liked. When the grey train pulled out of the station, the girl was gone.

'Seems there's going to be a bit of a delay,' Uncle Nat said, ushering Hal back to the stairs. 'Heavy snowfall has caused an accident. There's a bridge down. All trains are being redirected inland to avoid that section of track.'

'What does that mean?'

'Our train will be late arriving. However, the guard thinks it won't leave much later than timetabled. He said we should wait downstairs in the ticket hall, where it's warm. There'll be an announcement when it arrives.'

'Will we still be able to get to Abisko?'

'Yes, but our train will travel a longer route, to avoid the bridge. We'll arrive later than planned.'

Hal didn't think spending more time on the train was so bad.

At the foot of the stairs, on the busy concourse underneath the platforms, Uncle Nat found them a seat on a bench and left Hal with the bags while he ventured off in search of more coffee.

On the opposite benches was a group of people, each travelling with a different musical instrument. A short man with wild grey hair and expressive eyebrows was talking loudly, waving his hand.

While he waited for his uncle to return, Hal pulled out his sketchbook and drew the fascinating ensemble with their interestingly shaped luggage.

On the blank page he swiftly and loosely drew a series of eggs for heads, tipping them to the right angle, then he marked the ends and back of the bench and drew marks for knees and feet. He'd been practising drawing at speed for a year and a half now, and was able to get down all the important lines at a breakneck pace. At one end of the bench stood an instrument case the size of a man, and Hal immediately knew it had to be a double bass. It was strapped with a bungee cord to a little trolley. The man sat beside it was tall and cheery-looking. He had a thicket of tight corkscrew curls, and his arm was around the woman beside him. She had a cherubic face and long hair that draped over her shoulder. Her head was tipped against his chest while her arm lazily lay over a cello case between her knees. Hal guessed they were a couple. Next to them were three women chatting and laughing. The first woman had a mane of red hair flopped over her head revealing a shaved undercut. She had a black briefcase on her lap which Hal guessed was either for an oboe or a clarinet. It had a sticker on it that said *The Dynamic Dozen*. The capital *D*s were bass clefs and the *z* was a treble clef. The blonde girl giggling beside her had a violin case at her feet, and next to her was the girl who was telling the funny story. She had cat-eye glasses and curly hair that framed her mischievous moon face. The music case at her feet was large and strangely shaped. Hal wasn't sure what it was. It too had a sticker saying *The Dynamic Dozen*.

They must be a musical group travelling together, Hal thought as he drew, and wondered if they were waiting for the same train as him. The animated man with the wild grey hair was looking stressed as he talked excitedly to a wide-eyed elfin woman, and Hal guessed he was the band leader. Another man carrying a violin case came and stood beside him, and Hal added him to the picture.

'*Ritar du oss?*' said a woman's voice and Hal jumped.

He found himself looking up into the merry eyes of a woman with effortlessly punky thick black hair. She wore a leather jacket with the collar turned up and her lips were painted a purple that clashed with her brown skin.

'Er, sorry, I'm English,' Hal volunteered, blushing.

'I asked, are you drawing us?' The woman pointed to his picture.

'Oh. Yes. You don't mind, do you?'

'Not at all.' She sat down beside him on the bench. 'You are very good. And quick!'

'Thanks.'

'You have captured a perfect likeness of Gustav and Astrid.' She pointed at the bass and cello player. 'And here I see Klara, Julia and Siv.'

'What's the instrument in that case?' He pointed at the lumpen form in front of Siv.

'The French horn.'

'Do you play an instrument?'

'Yes.' She pulled two brass sticks from the inside pocket of her jacket and pushed the handles so that they became brushes. She beat them on his sketchbook. 'My name is Birgitta and I play percussion and piano.'

'Is the Dynamic Dozen a band?'

'We are the smallest symphony orchestra in the world,' Birgitta replied. 'Gustav plays bass, Astrid cello, Klara oboe,'

Julia violin, Siv French horn.' Hal hurriedly scribbled down their names and instruments beside their portraits. Birgitta pointed to the bench behind them where four men were sitting.

'Oscar clarinet, Stefan viola, Per bassoon, Anders flute.'
She turned towards the animated man with the wild grey mop and the elfin woman.
'Helena harp, and Magnus is our conductor . . .'

Birgitta (percussionist)

Stefan (viola)

Oscar (clarinet)

Per (bassoon)

Gustav (bass)

Astrid (cello)

She was going to say more, but Siv called out to her in Swedish and they exchanged words Hal couldn't understand.

'Are you travelling on the Narvik train?' Hal asked when she turned her attention back to him.

Helena (harp)

Magnus (conductor)

Anders (flute)

Klara (oboe)

Julia (violin)

Siv (french horn)

Birgitta nodded. 'We are going to Kiruna. On Sunday we play at the St Lucia Day Festival of Lights.'

'Oh! I'll be there then too. What's St Lucia Day?'

'The winter solstice. You must come. There's a parade, gingerbread, and lots of music. It marks the beginning of the Christmas season.'

'Oh, I'd like that. It sounds fun!'

'It is.' She smiled.

Uncle Nat returned carrying two cups, and Hal introduced him to Birgitta, who stood to let him sit down. They fell to talking about classical music, so Hal continued to work on his picture, slurping happily at his hot chocolate as he drew the Dynamic Dozen.

An announcement came over the tannoy in Swedish.

'Our train has arrived,' Birgitta told them. 'But it needs to be cleaned, we cannot board yet.'

'We can't board the train,' Hal said to his uncle, 'but I'd like to see the engine and maybe draw it.'

'Of course,' Uncle Nat said, getting to his feet and picking up his holdall. 'It was nice meeting you, Birgitta.'

Up on the platform, the air was bitingly cold, but Hal didn't feel it as he hurried to the front of the train, to see the locomotive that would pull him all the way to the Arctic Circle. She was mostly silver, with round porthole windows in her side, a square red nose and a snowplough shielding her undercarriage. A pantograph reached up to the electric wires above the tracks to power the train. Hal thought the engine looked sturdy and reassuring. He liked the circular lamps on her front, beneath the two rectangular windscreens; they made it look like the engine had rosy cheeks.

'They've opened the doors for passengers to board.' Uncle Nat looked at his watches. 'If we leave soon, we'll only be departing twenty minutes late.'

'I've got the outline. I can finish my picture on the train,' Hal said, snapping his sketchbook shut and feeling a thrill at the prospect of their epic journey. 'Let's go and find our compartment.'

As they walked back along the platform, Hal saw the Dynamic Dozen struggling aboard with their instruments. A flash of blue and red caught his eye, and he turned his head to find he was staring at the Sámi girl he'd seen in the Christmas market that morning. She noticed him looking at her and

turned away. Hal felt himself getting hot with embarrassment. He hadn't meant to be rude.

'This is us,' Uncle Nat said, grabbing the handle beside the silver steps and climbing on board. The light grey corridor was narrow, with a dark linoleum floor. The windows were framed with pine. Uncle Nat checked the numbers outside each compartment, until he found the one matching their ticket.

The compartment was small, but functional. On the right wall was a narrow red sofa that would convert into a bed, and above Hal's head a bunk had been made up with white sheets. A fold-out shelf suggested a third bunk could be added between the two. There was a corner sink below the window and enough floor space for two people to stand. A ladder was bolted to the left wall, and could be released using a hinge, allowing a person to climb into the top bunk.

'Room for three, but perfect for two,' said Uncle Nat, as Hal backed out of the compartment to let him remove his bag and coat.

There was a loud beeping sound as the train doors began to close. Hal heard a shout and looked out the window. A woman in a bobble hat and pink ski jacket came pelting up the platform stairs holding two full carrier bags in front of her. She leaped onto the train, vanishing from view as the carriage doors clicked shut.

Hal smiled to himself as the train slowly moved out of Stockholm Central Station. He was on his way to the Arctic!

CHAPTER SEVEN

THE SHADOW

Hal clambered up the ladder and onto his bunk. He was surprised at how roomy the compartment felt. It had a high ceiling, so he had plenty of room to sit cross-legged, and his bed was a few centimetres wider and longer than the sleeper trains he'd taken in the past. He wedged his rucksack into a storage space by his feet and took off his coat, pulling out his sketchbook and pens.

The lights of an office block slid past the window and Hal noticed how smooth the train's motion was. It was quiet too. He guessed the Swedish rail tracks must be welded together.

Uncle Nat removed some items from his holdall and lifted it into a luggage rack above the window. They exchanged contented smiles.

Hal marked the strong horizontal and vertical lines of the compartment onto a fresh page in his sketchbook, drawing his bird's-eye view of the room.

There was a knock on the door. Uncle Nat opened it.

'*God eftermiddag*, sir.' A smiling woman stood in the doorway wearing a uniform in the same colours as the train:

charcoal trousers, a light grey shirt and a red buttoned-up waistcoat. Her hair was pulled up into a neat bun above her heavily made-up face.

'Good afternoon,' Uncle Nat replied.

'You are English?'

'Yes.'

'You're a party of three?'

'Two.'

'Have you been informed of the diverted route and the new arrival times of the train?'

'Yes, I believe we're taking an inland route to avoid a damaged bridge?'

'This is correct.' She glanced up at Hal, who was inserting her into his drawing. 'Please listen for announcements. The driver will update you with new information when he gets it.'

'Thank you.' Uncle Nat nodded. 'We will.'

'The restaurant is now open for teas, coffees and dinner. My name is Inga. You can find me on the train if you need help with anything. I will check on you sometimes.'

'Thank you.' Uncle Nat closed the door and looked up at Hal. 'How is it up there?'

'Brilliant. I've got lots of room.' As he said this, Hal threw his arms out to demonstrate, and his sketchbook slid from his knees and tumbled off the bunk. Uncle Nat caught it before it could hit the ground. 'Whoops! Sorry!' Hal reached his hand down to retrieve the book, but Uncle Nat was staring at his picture of the Dynamic Dozen.

'This drawing.' His voice was a whisper.

'It's the musicians in the tiny orchestra.' Hal's stomach tightened at the expression on Uncle Nat's face. Something was wrong.

'It can't be,' Uncle Nat said to himself, slowly sitting on the red sofa.

'What's the matter?' Hal grabbed hold of the ladder and climbed down. 'Is there something wrong with my picture?'

'Everyone in this picture, you're sure they're all in the Dynamic Dozen?' Uncle Nat's face was ashen.

'Yes.' Hal sat down beside his uncle and looked at the drawing. 'Birgitta told me all their names and the instruments they played, but I've not finished the picture yet.'

'Who is this man?' Uncle Nat pointed to a man at the edge of the picture, beside Magnus the conductor and Helena the harpist.

'He's a violin player.' Hal pointed to the case beside him. 'Birgitta was about to tell me his name, but she got cut off.'

'You're sure?'

Hal was about to say yes, but then he thought for a moment. Was he sure? He looked back at the picture. 'They're called the Dynamic Dozen, right? And there are . . .' He counted them. 'Twelve musicians plus the conductor.' He looked enquiringly at his uncle. 'Why? Who do you think he is?'

'It can't be who I thought it was.' Uncle Nat leaned back. 'I'm sorry. Ignore me. I don't know what's got into me. It's been a strange day, what with Morti taking off like that, and then the pickpocket incident. I'm a little on edge. Do you know, when we were walking through Kungsträdgården, I felt like we were being followed.'

Hal sat bolt upright. 'I had the same feeling.'

'You did?'

'I didn't want to say anything in case it sounded stupid.'

'Neither did I!'

They stared at each other for a second, and then both laughed.

'What are we like?' Uncle Nat shook his head.

Hal pointed at the man in the picture. 'Who did you think this was?'

'It can't be him. The man I was thinking of is dead.'

'Dead?'

'He died a long time ago, when you were a baby. He was infamous, although not many people knew what he looked like. His identity was a closely guarded secret.'

'Who was he?'

'He was a hitman, an assassin, known as the Shadow.'

'An assassin?'

'Yes. He started his career as a French spy, but became a double agent, earning him the name Moucharder. It means *rat* in French.'

'Moucharder,' Hal repeated.

'When he was exposed as a double agent, selling secrets for money, he went to ground, hiding in England. Moucharder later resurfaced as a gun for hire and became known as "the Shadow". He was a deadly shot. They used to say, "You cannot outrun the Shadow." It is believed he was behind at least two assassinations during the Cold War.'

'How did he die?'

'He was shot and fell from a cliff into the sea.'

'How do you know?'

'Because . . .' Uncle Nat sighed. 'Because I was there when it happened.'

'You were?'

'The British government wanted a witness, a journalist,

who would write the story of how the Shadow was neutralized.'

'Neutralized?'

'Vanquished.'

'You mean killed, don't you?'

'Yes.' Uncle Nat looked ashamed. 'The Shadow walked into a trap. He was hired to assassinate someone, but when he turned up to do the job, there were people waiting for him.'

Hal looked down at the picture of the violin player. 'Do you really think this could be him?'

'His face is etched into my memory.' Uncle Nat's voice was a whisper.

'Why would he be playing violin with the Dynamic Dozen?'

'I don't know,' Uncle Nat admitted. 'He should be dead. But, if he isn't, and it is him . . .'

The silence that accompanied the look they exchanged was heavy with dread.

'What do we do?' Hal asked.

'The Shadow knows who I am. He knows what I look like. If he is alive and on this train, I can't leave the compartment. It could put both our lives in jeopardy.'

'You don't think he's after you?'

'I don't see how he could be.' Uncle Nat pushed his thumb and forefinger under his glasses and rubbed his eyes. 'But if he discovers I'm on the train . . .'

'Do you think he'd want revenge?' Hal's chest felt tight at the thought of anyone wanting to harm his uncle.

'Would you want revenge, if someone had been part of an attempt on your life?'

Hal studied his drawing trying to remember what the man had been doing in the ticket hall. 'This man can't be the Shadow. You have to be a really good musician to play violin professionally.'

'There's one way to know for certain. In the early part of his career, the Shadow was injured on an espionage mission for the French government. The top of his ear was taken off by a bullet. If the violin player has part of his ear missing, then we'll know he is the Shadow.' Uncle Nat puffed out a long breath. 'Look, Hal, we're only on this train until tomorrow afternoon. I think it would be best if we stay in our compartment until then.' He forced a smile, shoving his hand into his holdall. 'I brought a deck of cards.' He pulled out a box of playing cards. 'We could play gin rummy?'

'Wait, but the Shadow doesn't know who *I* am,' Hal said. 'I can go and get us food from the restaurant car. We're going to need dinner and breakfast. And, if I see the violin player, I can look at his ears.'

Uncle Nat frowned.

'My Plopp won't be enough food to keep us going until tomorrow afternoon.' Hal suppressed a chuckle at the name of the chocolate bar, but Uncle Nat didn't smile.

'I suppose, if you went now, the restaurant should be reasonably empty. Passengers will be settling into their compartments. It's a while till dinner.' He took a credit card from his wallet. 'Grab any food that looks tasty and get lots.

And if the violin player is there, stay away from him. Do you hear me? Don't so much as look at him.'

Hal nodded as he took the card. 'Is there anything you especially want?'

'I'll be happy with anything, but if there's reindeer stew, I'll have that.'

'Reindeer stew?' Hal stared at his uncle with horror. 'No one eats that!'

'Yes, they do. It's delicious and a common Swedish dish, especially in the north.' Uncle Nat smiled at the look on Hal's face. 'Reindeer meat is very lean and tasty. You should try it.'

'No, thanks.' Hal thought of Rudolph and the reindeers that pulled Father Christmas's sleigh. He'd never thought about them being edible!

Slipping his uncle's card into his pocket, Hal drew in a deep breath, told himself he was on a secret mission, and yanked the compartment door open. Every muscle in his entire body immediately froze as he found himself staring at a very familiar woman, with her fist raised about to knock.

'*Mum!*' Hal cried out.

CHAPTER EIGHT

THE MOTHER OF
ALL SHOCKS!

'Mum! Wh-what are you doing here?' Hal spluttered, feeling like he'd been doused in icy water.

'Bev!' Uncle Nat jumped to his feet. He looked as shocked as Hal was. 'Is everything all right?'

'I don't know!' Hal's mum said, looking from him to Hal and back again. 'Is it? Is everything all right? You tell me.' Her voice was shrill as she narrowed her eyes accusingly. 'Nat, why aren't you answering your mobile phone? I've been trying to call you since last night!'

'Oh dear,' Uncle Nat said, taking his sister's arm, pulling her into the compartment by the sleeve of her rustling pink ski jacket, and shutting the door. 'Come in, Bev. Sit down.' He lowered her onto the seat beside him. 'I'm so sorry. I didn't think. I lost my phone yesterday evening and I haven't had the chance to replace it.'

'You lost it?'

'Doing the funky chicken,' Hal said, waggling his arms, trying to lighten the mood.

'Surely me not answering my phone isn't the reason you've come all the way to Stockholm? Is it? Bev?'

Hal's mum grabbed him, wrapping her arms around him so tightly she squeezed the air out of his lungs. 'I came because . . . because . . . after you left me at the airport, when I was walking back to the car, I got this horrible feeling.'

Hal tried to disentangle himself. 'What horrible feeling?'

'I thought . . . I thought . . . I might never see you again.' Her lips trembled and her eyes filled with tears. 'You don't know what it's like.' She shook her head. 'Every time you go on one of these adventures, something terrible always happens, and this time . . . I just had this awful feeling that you might not come back.' She looked at Hal as if he were about to vanish in a puff of smoke.

'I'm fine, Mum,' Hal said. 'Really, I am. We've had a lovely day. Uncle Nat took me to a Christmas market this morning and we got you and Ellie a present.' He glanced at Uncle Nat, who had his head in his hands. 'Didn't we?'

'Yes.' Uncle Nat snapped his head up, getting a hold of himself, and trying to smile. 'Yes, we did, and Hal bought Colin some Plopp!'

'Plopp?'

'It's a type of chocolate!' Hal told her as he shinned up the ladder to his bunk, grabbed the paper bag from his rucksack and jumped down. He kneeled in front of his mum. 'Look, I got this horse for you, and a cute troll for Ellie. These guys are supposed to look after your home.'

Beverly Beck took the beautifully painted horse from her

son, hugging it to her chest, and burst into tears. 'I've been . . . so . . . worried,' she hiccupped. 'The premonition was so strong, and then when you didn't answer your phone . . .' She shook her head. 'I had to come. If anything happened to you, Hal, I'd never forgive myself.'

'Neither would I,' Uncle Nat said softly. He pulled a blue polka-dotted handkerchief from his pocket and offered it to her. 'But Bev, how on earth did you get here?'

'I nearly didn't.' She blew her nose loudly. 'I was too late to get on Hal's flight, and it was the last plane to Stockholm. I bought a ticket on the first available flight this morning. Then I rang Colin, told him what I was doing and moved my car to the long stay car park.'

'What did Dad say?' Hal asked, stunned by his mother's dramatic actions. He'd never known her be like this.

'Your dad believes in my funny feelings. It was one of my premonitions that resulted in us getting married. He's at home looking after Ellie and Bailey. I bought this hideous coat and bobble hat in the airport.' She looked apologetically at Uncle Nat and pulled her hat off, freeing her ash-blonde hair. 'I don't really have the right clothes for the Arctic.'

He patted her hand. 'Don't worry about that now.'

'I slept in the car and boarded the first plane they'd let me on. I got to Stockholm station as quickly as I could and bought a ticket for the train to Narvik. I almost didn't make it. The doors were beeping as I ran onto the platform.'

'That was you!' Hal said, realizing he'd seen his mum running for the train.

'But you did make it,' Uncle Nat said soothingly. 'You're here with us now, and we're all safe.'

'I did make it, didn't I?' Hal's mum looked astonished, and then to his surprise she burst out laughing. 'Oh!' She held her sides as she laughed. 'Oh, I'm sorry. It's just, I was so worried about you, Hal, and now . . . I feel a bit silly.'

'Well, it's lovely to have you with us.' Uncle Nat smiled and put his arm around his sister. 'And, as luck would have it, my friend Mortimer was meant to be travelling in the compartment next door. I booked her ticket. If you don't mind masquerading as Mortimer, you can have a whole compartment to yourself!'

'Really?' Hal's mum beamed. 'I could only afford a ticket in coach. I thought I'd have to sleep sitting up.'

'Hal was just on his way to the restaurant.' Uncle Nat shot him a meaningful look. 'Hal, why don't you grab some food for dinner, and if you can, a couple of cups of boiling water and sachets of milk. I think those Yorkshire Gold tea bags are needed now, don't you?'

Hal bolted out of the compartment. His head was spinning. His mum had never done anything like this before. It had freaked him out when she said she thought she'd never see him again. He'd heard her talk about her premonitions and always thought them silly, but if the man with the violin was the Shadow . . . were he and Uncle Nat in real danger? He gave an involuntary shiver. He mustn't think like this. He was letting feelings and suspicions rule his head. He needed to stick to what he trusted: logic and observation. Right now, nobody was in any danger. Uncle Nat had watched the Shadow fall to his death. The man with the violin was probably just a violin player.

When he reached the dining car, he was relieved to find it almost empty. It was set up like a canteen, with a counter leading to a till. Hal moved along the display of sandwiches and meals, choosing two roasted chicken breast and vegetable meals for himself and Mum, and a reindeer stew for Uncle Nat. He loaded his tray, getting the hot water and milk for the tea, and then paid with Uncle Nat's card at the till.

As he stood waiting for the cafe attendant to heat up the food, Birgitta strolled into the carriage through the far door. 'Hey, Picasso,' she greeted him, as she headed for the coffee machine.

'Hi.' Hal took the hot food from the attendant, stacking it on the tray. 'Birgitta, can I ask you a question?

'Shoot.' She nodded, adding milk to her drink.

'You know you're called the Dynamic Dozen . . . ? Are there twelve of you plus a conductor?'

'There are twelve of us *including* Magnus. He's not only a conductor. He plays trumpet too.'

'How many violins do you have?' Hal asked, feeling sick.

'One. Julia.' She tilted her head. 'Why?'

'Oh, nothing.' Hal found he was struggling to breathe. 'I counted wrong when I did the drawing. I thought there were thirteen of you. Two violins.'

'That wouldn't be a dozen, would it?' Birgitta teased.

'No.' Hal attempted to smile. His heart was thumping. 'I'd better get back to my uncle.' He picked up his tray. 'See you later.'

If the man in the picture wasn't with the Dynamic Dozen . . . ? Hal tried to calm his jangling mind as he carried the tray carefully through the train. The man with the violin could be anyone. He might not even have boarded this train. But what if he *was* the Shadow? Was he still an assassin? Was he on a mission? Did he have a target? What was in that violin case? Had he seen Uncle Nat? And how was Hal going to tell his uncle without Mum realizing what they were talking about?

Questions buzzed around Hal's skull like angry bees. He tapped the compartment door with his foot and arranged a smile on his face. 'Reindeer stew is served,' he said cheerily, as the door opened.

CHAPTER NINE

THIRD WHEEL

Hal's mum was sitting upright on the sofa, propped up on cushions, with her legs out in front of her, covered in a red fleece blanket. She had calmed down, although the wooden horse Hal had given her was tucked under her arm and her eyes were red and swollen. She smiled when he entered with the tray of food and drinks. Uncle Nat set about making the tea on the side of the circular sink. Hal perched at his mum's feet.

'Well, this is exciting,' she declared. 'I've always wondered what it would be like to come along with you two on one of your train adventures.' She smiled at Hal. 'Do you think we'll find a crime that needs solving?'

'No sign of one yet,' Hal lied, immediately feeling intensely guilty. To change the subject, he pointed to the window. 'Look, it's really snowing now.' His mum smiled, and Hal thought with dismay that he didn't want to be treated like he was at home, like a kid. Would Uncle Nat treat him differently now? Would he stop him from trying to discover if the Shadow was on the train? This day was going from bad to worse.

'Thanks, Nat.' Hal's mum sighed happily as Uncle Nat passed her a cardboard cup of tea. 'I can't believe I'm here. Do you know, I've wanted to see the Northern Lights since I was a little girl?' She looked wistful when she said this. 'I got a bit jealous when Hal said you were going to see them together.'

'You should have said, Bev,' Uncle Nat scolded gently. 'I would have invited you along. I thought you were busy with Ellie and work.'

'I am. It's been a hard juggle, going back to teaching, with Ellie being so little.' His mum blew away the steam drifting from her tea and took a sip. 'There's never enough time for everything.' She looked at Hal. 'I wish we did more things together. Your relationship with your uncle is wonderful.' She glanced at Nat. 'I'm happy you're such good friends and have adventures together, but –' she gave a tiny shrug – 'sometimes I feel a bit left out.'

Hal was astonished. It hadn't occurred to him that his mother envied his trips with Uncle Nat. She always seemed to be so busy and stressed.

'Well, you're with us now,' Uncle Nat said, putting the tray with her boxed meal and a set of wooden cutlery onto her lap. 'So, eat up.'

'Yes, sir.' She laughed, lifting the lid and tucking into her dinner. 'I really am actually going to the Arctic, aren't I?' Her eyes shone.

'Yes, Bev, you are.'

Hal glanced at Uncle Nat, silently pleading, trying to

communicate using only the power of thought that he urgently needed to talk to him.

'Bev, after you've eaten, I really think you should have a nap,' Uncle Nat said. 'You must be exhausted.'

'I really am,' she replied, and she yawned.

'Hal and I will go and take our food to the dining car. Let you rest for a bit.' Uncle Nat held out Hal's box of food and picked up his own. He glanced meaningfully at Hal's sketchbook, indicating he should bring it. 'We'll come back in an hour and see how you're feeling. Then we'll get your things and set you up in Morti's compartment.'

'Are you sure?' Bev replied, looking grateful for the offer. 'I don't want to be in the way. I promised myself I wouldn't cramp your style.'

'Don't be silly. Get some rest. We've got a snowy adventure into the Arctic ahead of us. You're going to need your strength.'

'You're not in the way, Mum,' Hal said.

'Thank you, pet.'

They exited the compartment and walked in silence to the next carriage.

'We can't go to the dining car,' Hal whispered.

'We're not going to,' Uncle Nat replied under his breath. 'We could have used Morti's compartment, but we can't risk Bev hearing us through the wall. This carriage has larger compartments, with six berth couchettes,' he muttered, as Hal peered through the glass doors. 'Look. This one's empty.'

Hal followed his uncle inside, drawing the red curtains across the door behind them for privacy. They set their food boxes onto the shallow table under the window and sat down opposite each other. For a long moment there was no sound but the squeak and rumble of the train carriage.

'I saw Birgitta in the restaurant,' Hal said, in a low voice. 'The man in my picture –' he pulled out the sketchbook – 'is not in the Dynamic Dozen. They only have one violin player and she is a woman called Julia.'

'I see.' Uncle Nat looked pensive as he thought through their predicament.

'What are we going to do about Mum?' Hal hissed.

'Nothing. The way I see it, we're on this train until tomorrow afternoon,' Uncle Nat reasoned. 'All I have to do is stay hidden, in the compartment.' He took the lid off his food tray. 'I can say I'm feeling ill. Nothing too serious. A twenty-four-hour complaint. I'll say I've got a stomach upset.' He forked stew into his mouth.

'That'll be because you're eating a reindeer,' Hal said, and Uncle Nat snorted. 'But what about the Shadow?'

'Look.' Uncle Nat pointed his fork at Hal's sketch. 'We don't know if this man *is* the Shadow. We don't even know if he got on this train.'

'I haven't seen him.'

'Exactly,' Uncle Nat agreed. 'We mustn't panic.'

'And Mum?'

'If you and I are ever going to be allowed to travel together again, I think we're going to have to keep our fears about the Shadow a secret.'

Hal nodded, and they ate their food in silence for a bit.

'But if that man *is* the Shadow, and he *did* get on this train . . .' Hal looked up. 'He might be planning to kill someone?'

'I wish I'd never seen your drawing.' Uncle Nat shook his head. 'You know, I'm probably mistaken. The Shadow is dead. I shouldn't have said anything.' He looked Hal straight in the eyes. 'We're on this train taking a family trip to visit the Arctic and see the Northern Lights for Christmas. Hal, we can't get involved. Do you understand?'

Hal looked out of the window into the darkness, past the blizzard of snow, and didn't reply.

CHAPTER TEN

UNSETTLED

On their way back, Hal heard a baby crying. The noise was coming from the compartment next to Morti's empty one. Through the open doorway Hal saw a man with a baby in one arm and a nappy in his mouth, struggling to unzip a bag on the floor. 'Do you need a hand?'

'Sorry for the crying,' he mumbled.

'Don't worry,' Hal replied. 'I have a baby sister. Here, let me help you.' He paused to make sure he wasn't trespassing, but the man's grateful smile told him it was OK to step into the compartment. Hal opened the zip of the bag and pulled out a packet of bottom wipes.

'*Tack, tack.*' The man took them, and found he now had a nappy between his teeth, a baby in one arm, wet wipes in the other hand, and was unable to move. He looked momentarily perplexed, then handed the baby to Hal. 'Would you hold Alfred for me?'

Taking the wailing bundle, Hal hugged the baby to his shoulder, like he used to do with Ellie when she was smaller.

He bounced Alfred up and down, taking in the state of the compartment. There was a baby bottle half-full of milk in the sink. A packet of nappies was ripped open, a few were scattered across the bunk, and the bag on the floor had baby clothes exploding out of it. Alfred let out a loud burp and immediately stopped crying.

Alfred's father, who was laying down a towel on the bottom bunk to make a changing mat, beamed at the sound, looking delighted. 'You are good with babies.'

'I help my mum with my sister, Ellie. She's one and a half now.'

Taking little Alfred from Hal, the man laid him on the towel. 'Your sister is very lucky to have a big brother such as you . . .'

'My name's Hal.'

'Mine is Erik.' He unfastened Alfred's babygro. 'You are from England?'

'Yes, my uncle and I are travelling to Abisko to see the Northern Lights.' Hal pointed out to the corridor where Uncle Nat was politely hanging back. The two men exchanged a nod. Hal remembered his mum sleeping in their compartment and added, 'With my mum too.'

'We are on our way home. We've been to visit little Alfred's *farmor* and *farfar* – his grandparents – in Stockholm. We live in Kiruna. I work in the mine there.'

'It's one of the largest iron-ore mines in the world, isn't it?' Uncle Nat asked. 'I heard it's so big, the ground underneath the town is collapsing.'

'Yes. They are moving all the important buildings in Kiruna five kilometres down the road – some brick by brick.' He opened Alfred's nappy and wrinkled his nose.

'Fascinating,' Uncle Nat replied.

'You mustn't worry about Alfred crying,' Hal said, retreating to the corridor. 'My mum's in the compartment next door and we're the next one along. We always bring earplugs when we travel on sleeper trains.'

'Yes, we won't mind,' Uncle Nat agreed.

'That is kind.' Erik smiled, and turned to deal with Alfred's loaded nappy, saying over his shoulder, 'I hope the Northern Lights dance for you.'

Hal's mum was wide awake when they entered the compartment.

'I heard a baby crying,' she said. 'I'm that used to getting up for Ellie, it woke me.'

'There's a baby called Alfred in the compartment next to yours,' Hal said, sitting beside her.

'Did you manage to sleep?' Uncle Nat asked.

'I dozed, but I feel much better.' She swung her legs round to sit up. 'Did you explore the train while I slept?'

'Er, no . . . we just ate our food in the restaurant,' Hal replied.

'Great.' His mum rubbed her hands together. 'Let's all do it together.'

Hal flashed Uncle Nat a worried look.

'That is what you usually do, isn't it?' his mum asked. 'You visit the loco before departure, draw it, and then once you're on the train you explore it. That's what you told me you do.'

'Yes . . .' Hal replied. 'That is what we normally do. It's just that, so far, this hasn't been a normal trip, because *you* burst into our compartment after we left Stockholm.'

She laughed.

Uncle Nat put one hand on his stomach and winced.

'Are you feeling OK, Uncle Nat?' Hal asked.

'I'm not sure.' Uncle Nat paused, opened his mouth, then closed it, looking embarrassed. 'I may need to go to, er . . . visit the bathroom.' He winced again and Hal reflected, not for the first time, that his uncle was a shockingly good liar.

'Oh!' His mum jumped up. 'Well, er . . . why don't I take Hal to explore the train? Give you a bit of space?'

'Would you mind?' Uncle Nat grimaced as he hung his head, giving her a pathetic smile. 'This is a bit embarrassing.'

'Not at all. Come on, Hal.'

'I told him not to eat reindeers,' Hal said as his mum opened the compartment door and Uncle Nat gave him an almost imperceptible wink.

'We have to walk through the whole train, to the locomotive,' Hal said to his mum.

As they passed Erik's compartment, the door was still open. Hal could see Alfred was on his knee, sucking on the bottle from the sink. 'Erik, this is my mum.'

'Beverly,' she clarified, with a smile and a little wave. 'Pleased to meet you.' She tilted her head. 'Ahhh, look at him! Little angel,' she cooed at Alfred.

Hal pulled her away, carrying on to the end of the corridor, where there was a toilet and a shower room, beside a deep shelved recess in the wall for luggage. The yellow strip lights above their heads cast grubby shadows and he was uncomfortably aware of how easily a person might wait there, unseen, if they wanted to ambush a passing passenger.

'Oh Hal, don't let me forget to pick up my bags from the rack in coach.'

'We can get them on the way back through the train.' Hal wrenched open the heavy connecting door, and his nostrils filled with the acrid smell of the coupling corridor. He had to shout over the roar of the train. 'Once we've reached the front,

74

we'll turn around and walk all the way to the back of the train. I counted before we boarded. After the loco, there are nine carriages in total.'

'Then what do you do?' Beverly put her hand against the wall. The rocking of the train was making her unsteady on her feet.

'I draw it,' Hal replied, noting that this carriage was another sleeping car of three-berth compartments like their own. He pointed to his sketchbook sticking out of his pocket. 'I like doing train layout diagrams.'

'Hal, I hope you're not upset that I've hijacked your holiday. I was in such a state about getting to you, I didn't think about what would happen when I got here. When I saw that you were perfectly fine, I felt a bit . . . foolish.'

'It's all right,' Hal replied, as they ambled through the carriage with the six-berth compartments. He glanced into the one he and Uncle Nat had eaten in as they passed it. It was still empty. 'But you don't need to worry. Uncle Nat is really good at looking after me.'

'I'm sure he is, but I really had no choice. I can't explain it. I was overcome with this feeling that if I didn't find you, something bad would happen.' She shuddered. 'One day, if you have children, you may understand how terrifying a feeling that is.'

'I would be scared too if I thought I wasn't going to see you again.'

'Well, we're together now, and I'm happy we are.' His mum reached her arm round Hal's shoulders and gave him a squeeze. 'You can teach me to be a proper traveller like you and Nat.'

They passed into a coach carriage, seats lining the aisle in pairs. His mum pointed at two carrier bags in the luggage rack. 'Those are mine.'

'What's in them?'

'Socks, pants, toothbrush, toothpaste, deodorant, that kind of thing. I bought it all in rather a hurry at the airport. I couldn't find any thermals, and all I've got to wear is this.' She opened her arms and looked down at herself. 'I'm a bit worried I'll freeze to death once we get to the Arctic.'

'I'm sure there'll be shops in Kiruna,' Hal reassured her. 'We can get you some proper snow clothes there.'

They entered the dining car, which was now thronging with hungry passengers. Passing through the canteen, they headed into the eating area when Hal suddenly halted.

Sitting by himself at a table, wearing a black polo neck and rectangular glasses, looking at his phone and nursing a cup of coffee, was the man from his drawing. The man with the violin. The one Uncle Nat had recognized as the Shadow.

CHAPTER ELEVEN

THE DYNAMIC DOZEN

Hal's mum bumped into his back. 'What is it?'

'Oh, er . . . n-nothing,' Hal stammered, quickly visualizing the lines he would draw to capture a detailed portrait of the man in front of him. 'It's just, I never asked Uncle Nat if he wanted us to bring him a drink. You know, to help with his tummy troubles.'

'That's considerate.' His mum smiled. 'Fizzy water's good for an upset stomach. We'll grab him a bottle on our way back.'

Hal nodded, moving slowly, trying not to stare too obviously at the stranger as he approached the table. He could see the man's right ear; it was whole. But he couldn't see the left ear. As they were passing, Hal swayed, as if coping with the movement of the train, and affected a stumble against his table. The man turned his head to look at Hal. Hal's heart was thumping, but then he saw the man's left ear. It was whole. This man couldn't be the Shadow! A smile burst across his face. 'Oops! Sorry!'

Surprised to find a boy beaming happily at him, the man's eyebrows lifted above his glasses, and he returned the smile.

Hal felt lighter than air as he took his mum into the next carriage. Uncle Nat was mistaken. There was no assassin! He was safe. They could enjoy the journey without fear.

The next coach carriage had a curious glass compartment in the middle. As they passed, Hal saw it had a picture of a dog on the door. Inside was a handsome Alsatian sat obediently beside their owner, an elderly gentleman. 'They have dog-friendly compartments in Sweden!' he marvelled.

'We could do with those in the UK,' his mum replied. 'Then you could take Bailey on a train.'

After another carriage of six-berth rooms, there were two more with three-berth compartments like their own. The train's formation was a mirror image, with the dining car at the centre. In the final carriage, which abutted the engine, all the doors to the compartments were open. Hal heard the high trill of a flute and someone plucking a violin. The entire carriage was occupied by the Dynamic Dozen.

'Hey, Hal!' came a shout. Hal turned to see Birgitta sitting on the floor of the first compartment, a pair of drumsticks in her hands. Klara, the oboe player, was sitting on the bottom bunk, her instrument case open in front of her. She was cleaning the separate parts of her oboe with a long fluffy stick. Birgitta executed a drum roll on the floor. 'Welcome to the noisy carriage.'

His mum looked at Hal in surprise, curious to know how he came to be on first-name terms with the drummer.

'I'm exploring the train with my mum. Mum, this is Birgitta.'

'Beverly – pleased to meet you.' His mum smiled. 'How do you know Hal?'

'He drew us in the station,' Birgitta replied. 'He's a really good artist.'

'I can't take credit for that.' His mum looked proudly at him.

'There's talk of us playing a gig in the dining car,' Birgitta said to Hal. 'An impromptu concert. Tonight. You should come.'

Hal nodded enthusiastically. 'I'd love to hear you play!'

'One of the benefits of being the smallest symphony orchestra in the world is that we can all fit up one end of a train carriage.' Birgitta laughed. 'We're going to play in about an hour, once everyone has finished eating, around eight o'clock.'

'We'll be there,' Hal said.

Wanting to be certain the Shadow was not in any way part of the Dynamic Dozen, Hal made a mental note that the first two compartments in this carriage were occupied by Birgitta and Klara, then Julia – the violin player – and Siv, with her French horn. Further on were Anders the flautist, Stefan the viola player, and Per the bassoonist, playing cards on the sofa, while Oscar practised scales on his clarinet in the next compartment. Beyond them were the couple: Astrid the cellist with Gustav the bass player. Hal guessed that Helena the harpist and Magnus, the conductor and trumpet player, had the room with the closed door beside them.

Beyond the toilet and shower room, the window in the locked connecting door showed the dark metal rear of the locomotive. They had reached the end of the train.

'That's it. This is as far as we can go.' Hal looked at his mum. 'Ready to go back?'

'Yes. We'll get that fizzy water for Nat, and I could do with another cup of tea.'

'I'll bet he's feeling better,' Hal said, eager to tell Uncle Nat that the violin man wasn't the Shadow and that he could come out of the compartment. 'He might want to come and hear the concert.'

'He might, but let's not put too much pressure on him. A stomach upset is a horrid thing.'

On the way back they were carrying tea, biscuits, fizzy water and the two carrier bags of his mum's things, so Hal suggested they needn't explore the last carriage of the train, the one beyond theirs, as it was another sleeper car, and, although it would be nice to look out of the back window at the track and the snow, there wasn't much point, because it was too dark outside to see anything.

Uncle Nat was sitting up in his bunk, reading. As they came in, Hal saw his hand quickly cover his belly and he slumped a little.

'How are you feeling, pet?' His mum held out the bottle of fizzy water. 'We thought this might help settle your stomach.'

'We've explored the whole train,' Hal said meaningfully, fixing his uncle with a stare. 'In the dining car I saw that man who I thought was in the Dynamic Dozen.' He leaned forward.

'I don't know how I made that mistake, he didn't look like he had an *ear* for music, although *his ears were completely normal.*' Hal pointed to his own ears for emphasis.

'I met the Dynamic Dozen,' his mum said. 'They're staying in the first carriage. Birgitta told us they're playing a concert in the dining car after dinner tonight. Hal thought, if you were feeling better, you might like to come with us.'

Hal nodded enthusiastically and gave his uncle a thumbs-up.

'How lovely,' Uncle Nat replied. 'I am feeling a bit better, actually.'

'Have you been to the bathroom?' his mum asked.

'Er, no . . .' Uncle Nat looked embarrassed by the question.

'Ah . . .' Beverly nodded knowledgably. 'Probably trapped wind. Well, you know . . . better out than in.'

Uncle Nat blushed and Hal giggled.

'Shall we move your things next door?' Uncle Nat suggested. 'Get you settled in Morti's compartment?'

The two of them left, and Hal climbed the ladder to his bunk. Taking out his sketchbook, he drew the man he'd seen in the dining car, and then marked out a diagram of the train layout.

At five to eight, they got themselves ready to return to the dining car. Hal was looking forward to seeing Birgitta and the others play. Uncle Nat clambered up the ladder to get to his holdall, which was stowed in the luggage rack above the sink.

'Are you sure it's safe?' he asked in a soft voice.

'Yes.' Hal held up the portrait he'd done of the man in the

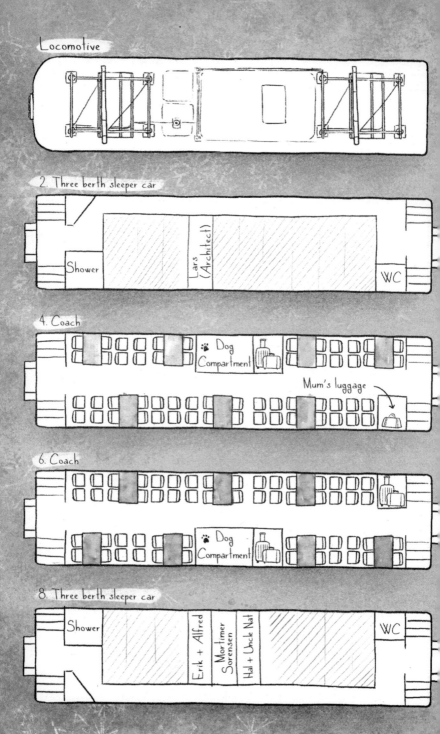

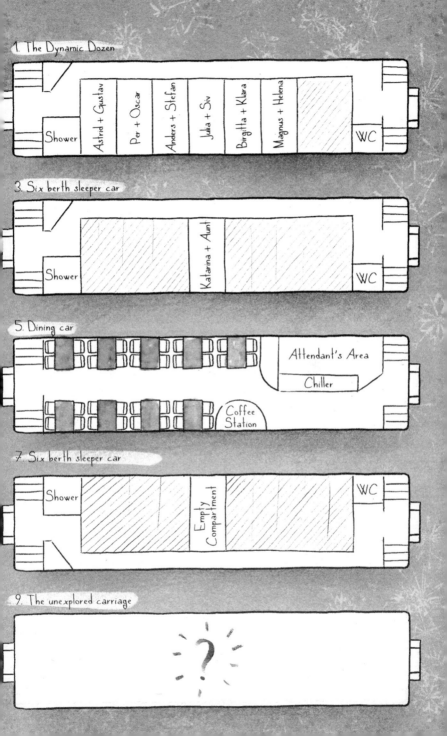

1. The Dynamic Dozen

Shower | Astrid + Gustav | Per + Oscar | Anders + Stefan | Julia + Siv | Birgitta + Klara | Magnus + Helena | | WC

3. Six berth sleeper car

Shower | Katarina + Aunt | WC

5. Dining car

Attendant's Area

Chiller

Coffee Station

7. Six berth sleeper car

Shower | Empty Compartment | WC

9. The unexplored carriage

?

dining car. 'This is him. He has normal ears. He even gave me a friendly smile.'

'His resemblance to the Shadow is uncanny,' Uncle Nat observed, pulling out a beanie hat from his holdall and pulling it on.

There was a tap at the door. 'Are you ready to go?' came his mum's voice.

'One second,' Uncle Nat replied, climbing back down. He took his glasses off. 'I might leave these here. I don't need my glasses to listen to music.'

As they filed out of the compartment, Hal whispered to his uncle, 'What's with the hat and no glasses?'

'Purely a precautionary measure,' Uncle Nat replied under his breath, and Hal realized it was a form of disguise.

CHAPTER TWELVE

THE RESTAURANT RECITAL

The dining car was filling up when they arrived. The Dynamic Dozen had gathered at the far end. The six woodwind and brass players were seated at a table to the right of the aisle; the strings and percussion were to the left. Everyone was squashed together, jostling their instruments, trying to find room to play.

Hal and his mum slipped into two free seats opposite Erik, cuddling Alfred against his chest, and a woman who introduced herself as Heidi. Alfred was clutching her finger as she pointed to each of the musical instruments and named them. Uncle Nat hovered at the edge of the table as Hal's mum and Heidi fell to talking about babies. Hal's mum put her arm around him, saying he was her baby, and plucked his sketchbook from his hand, proudly showing Heidi his drawings.

Magnus, the conductor, stood up, a baton in one hand, his trumpet in the other, indicating they were ready to start. Gustav took his double bass and went to stand with his back to the carriage door, so no one could walk through. Astrid moved her cello into the aisle, holding it between her knees. Birgitta kneeled down, setting out a glockenspiel, drum, and pair of hand cymbals on the floor. She looked up, spotted Hal and waved.

'Good evening, ladies and gentlemen,' Magnus said. 'We are the Dynamic Dozen, the world's smallest symphony orchestra. We thought, to make this journey memorable, we'd perform a short concert for you this evening.'

Everyone clapped. Hal looked over his shoulder and saw that there were passengers standing in the canteen and the cafe attendant had come out from behind the till. At a table across the aisle was the girl from the Christmas market, sitting beside the woman he assumed to be her mother. Hal caught her looking at him, but she turned away before he could smile. He wanted to say hello and ask her about reindeer, but he got the impression he wouldn't get a warm response.

'Here . . .' Hal got up. 'Uncle Nat, you take my seat. I want to draw.' He sat himself down in the aisle, pleased to have escaped the baby talk, and laid his sketchbook and pens on the floor. The girl in blue was behind his right shoulder now. If she looked, she'd see him drawing. Maybe that would spark a conversation.

Magnus turned his back to the audience with his left arm raised, baton hovering. It jerked to four silent counts, then swept downwards. The musicians with stringed instruments started plucking rhythmically. Birgitta, clutching four beaters, two in each fist, picked out a pretty, Christmassy tune on the glockenspiel.

Hal's mum clasped her hands together, and Uncle Nat

smiled at her. 'It's "The Dance of the Sugar Plum Fairy",' she whispered, as Per played a descending run of low notes on his bassoon. Oscar on clarinet, Klara on oboe, and Anders on flute, all joined in. Somehow Magnus seemed to have set the tempo of the music to match the rhythmic clatter of the train. There was a section of rippling notes played on the harp balanced in Helena's lap, and then the tune returned to Birgitta on her glockenspiel. Everyone listened in silence. Hal was so spellbound by the music that his pen hovered above his sketchbook throughout the piece. He didn't draw a line. At the end, the carriage exploded with applause.

The noise startled baby Alfred. He started to cry. Heidi fussed over him, taking him and rocking him gently. When the second piece of music began, Alfred immediately fell silent, and Hal drew.

The Dynamic Dozen played for forty minutes. At the end, as everyone applauded and cheered, Hal scrambled to his feet, grabbing up his sketchbook, making his way to Birgitta. 'That was brilliant!'

'You liked the music?'

'I loved it.' Hal nodded enthusiastically. 'What was the second one? The one that got faster and faster. It was mad.'

'Ha! That's from *Peer Gynt* by Grieg. It's called "In the Hall of the Mountain King".'

'I liked the bit where you kept crashing the cymbals.'

Birgitta introduced Hal to the rest of the orchestra, and they crowded round to see the picture he'd drawn of them playing, clapping him on the back and praising his skill.

When Hal returned to his mum and Uncle Nat, they were chatting with Heidi and Erik. His mum was playing peekaboo with Alfred. The crowd in the carriage was thinning, now that the concert was over. Feeling someone looking at him, Hal turned and met the eyes of the Sámi girl. Boldly taking a step in her direction, he said, 'I'm Hal, what's your name?'

The girl stared at him without blinking for a long moment. 'Katarina.'

'I saw you in the Christmas market in Stockholm, didn't I?'

She nodded and pointed to his sketchbook.

'What did you draw?'

'The orchestra. Do you want to see?' He opened it and showed her the picture.

'You did that?' She looked disbelievingly at the drawing.

'I drew you earlier.' Hal slid into the now vacant seat across the table from her. 'Look.' He flipped the pages back to the sketch he'd done of the Christmas market.

'Oh!' Katarina was surprised to see herself on the page. She pointed to a figure in the background. 'There is the thief that was following you.'

Hal peered at the picture and saw that Katarina was right. The woman who'd tried to pick Uncle Nat's pocket was in the background of his picture. He hadn't noticed.

'You must see lots of thieves stealing from people at the Christmas market.'

'No.' Katarina laughed. 'Stockholm is the safest city in Europe. There are hardly ever any crimes.' Hal frowned. 'This woman did not pick any other pockets, just your father's.'

'He's my uncle.'

Katarina smiled. 'I am travelling with my aunt.'

'You say the thief was following us?' Hal's pulse quickened. His and Uncle Nat's intuition had been right.

'She came into the market behind you. I watched her follow you around. She pretended to look at stalls, but she didn't buy anything. She kept looking at you two. When you went to get drinks, she walked into your uncle on purpose. Then you slapped her hand.' An impressed look crossed Katarina's face. 'That was good. But then she ran away. I didn't see her after that.'

Hal felt unsettled by Katarina's tale. He made a mental note to talk to his uncle about it.

'Why would someone follow you?' Katarina asked. 'Who are you?'

'No one.' Hal shrugged. 'But my uncle and I sometimes solve crimes together. We're detectives.'

'Detectives?' Katarina's expression was a mixture of interest and scepticism. 'Are you solving a crime right now?'

'Er . . .' Hal thought of Morti's burglary, and all the strange things that had happened to him in Stockholm. Until that moment, he hadn't thought that they could be connected, but what if they were? With a sinking feeling he realized it was too late. He'd left Morti's mystery behind in Stockholm. 'Not right now . . .' He reached for something else to talk about. 'My uncle says that Sámi people herd reindeer. Do you have reindeer? I love reindeer. I think they're brilliant.' He groaned inwardly as he heard himself gabbling.

Katarina's eyebrows shot up at this sudden change in conversation. 'Yes.'

'I've never seen a real reindeer, but I want to.'

'Oh.' There was an awkward pause.

'Hal!' Uncle Nat called over to him. 'Come and meet Lars.'

Hal saw that his uncle was talking to the man in the black polo neck whom they'd thought was the Shadow.

'I'd better go,' Hal said to Katarina. 'How far are you going on the train? We're going to Abisko.'

'I live in Jukkasjärvi, just outside Kiruna. That is where I get off,' replied Katarina.

'I might come and find you later. You can tell me about your reindeer.'

'If you want. We are in a six bed compartment that way.' She pointed.

As Hal left the table and went to stand by his uncle, he wondered if his deluge of reindeer questions had offended her.

'Lars, this is Hal,' Uncle Nat said.

'Hello.' Hal shook Lars's hand. 'I bumped into you earlier today.'

'Lars is an architect,' Uncle Nat said, seeming very pleased. 'He works at the Ice Hotel in Kiruna.'

'We're visiting there after we've been to Abisko, aren't we?' Hal said, and Uncle Nat nodded. 'How do you build a hotel out of ice?' he asked Lars.

'Over and over again,' Lars replied, with a chuckle. 'It melts every year in summer. And every winter, we build it again.'

Hal could tell from Uncle Nat's relaxed expression that he was delighted that this man was not the dreaded Shadow.

'What did you think of the concert?' Hal asked Lars.

'Magnificent!' Lars exclaimed. 'What talent they all have. I wish I could play an instrument. The only instrument I pick up every day is a pencil.'

Uncle Nat nodded. 'The architect's instrument.'

'It's getting late. I'm tired,' Hal's mum said, looking at him. 'Bedtime, I think.'

Hal wanted to protest about being sent to bed. Uncle Nat never did it, but it felt like a childish complaint to make, and his mum looked exhausted, so he said nothing.

'What a magical evening!' Hal's mum enthused as they all made their way back to their compartments. 'Yesterday, I could never have imagined that today I'd be on a train to the Arctic listening to the "Sugar Plum Fairy" played by the smallest orchestra in the world!'

'That's the best thing about having adventures on trains,' Hal said. 'You never know who you're going to meet or what's going to happen.'

'I had a really interesting conversation with Heidi about the Swedish education system,' his mum said. 'She's a teacher like me, you know. She says they don't send their children to school until they're six in Sweden. She and Erik make such a cute couple, and little Alfred is just adorable.'

While they'd been gone, their compartments had been turned down for the evening, and the red sofas had been transformed into beds.

Hal's mum wished them both goodnight, before going into her compartment. Hal clambered up the ladder and changed into his pyjamas. A few minutes later there was a knock on the door.

'Nat, I've lost my wedding ring!' His mum sounded worried. Hal peered over the bunk. 'It was on my hand this morning, but I don't remember when I last saw it.' She held up her left hand. 'It's gone.' She began fretfully searching the compartment. 'It must've come loose because my fingers are cold. It's never come off before.'

'When did you last have it?' Uncle Nat asked.

'I don't remember,' she wailed, looking up. 'Oh, Hal, your father's going to be so upset with me.'

'I'm sure we'll find it,' said Uncle Nat reassuringly. 'It's got to be here somewhere.'

The three of them searched the compartment, but found nothing.

'Whose are these?' Hal's mum asked, pulling Morti's keys out of one of Uncle Nat's shoes.

'They're the keys for Morti's cabin in Kiruna. We're staying there on Sunday night.'

'You can't keep them in a shoe! They should be kept somewhere safe.'

'I thought my shoe was safe,' Uncle Nat replied quietly.

'I'll look after them,' Hal's mum said, putting them into her pocket and zipping it up.

'I'll go back to the dining car and look for the ring,' said Uncle Nat. 'I'll tell the attendant on the till about it in case someone hands it in, and if I see Inga, I'll tell her too.'

'I'll help,' said Hal, scrambling out of his bed, thinking he might be able to sneak in a quick visit to Katarina.

'No, young man.' His mum stopped him. 'It's well past your bedtime. You need your sleep. You're still growing.'

Hal stiffened. He didn't like being talked to like this, but he held his tongue.

Uncle Nat winked at him as he opened the compartment door. 'I'll be back in a bit.'

Heidi was standing in the corridor and, seeing her, Hal's mum followed Uncle Nat out into the corridor, shutting the door behind her.

Hal heard their muffled conversation. It sounded like his mum and Heidi had gone into her compartment. He lay back in his bunk. The rhythm of the moving train brought back the music he'd heard that evening. He thought about how, even though he was lying still, he was moving ever closer towards the Arctic. He wondered how long it would take for Uncle Nat to search the dining car. He was anxious to tell him what Katarina had seen in the Christmas market that morning. He felt uneasy about it. Who was the woman who'd been following them? Why had she tried to steal Uncle Nat's wallet? Had there been something happening around them that they hadn't noticed? Maybe he hadn't imagined that noise in their hotel room. Where had Morti vanished to? His eyelids felt heavy. He let them close just for a second.

CHAPTER THIRTEEN

MORNING SHADOWS

As he woke, Hal sat up. *I'm in the Arctic!*

The compartment was dark, and the window blind was down. He leaned his head out over the edge of the bunk. Uncle Nat was fast asleep below him. A burning desire to see what the Arctic looked like meant Hal was immediately wide awake. He grabbed his sketchbook and pens, pulled on a pair of socks and, stealthy as a cat, climbed down the ladder and slipped out the compartment door.

A grey, unearthly light flooded through the windows of the corridor. Outside, he saw a strange and beautiful ghost world of black trees, white ground and hovering mist under a mushroom-coloured sky. Hal checked his watch. It was five thirty in the morning. The train was silent, devoid of people's chatter, footsteps or closing doors.

When he reached the dining car, Hal was the only passenger in it. The digital display on the wall told him that the temperature outside was minus eleven. He got himself some muesli with loganberries and a hot chocolate, paying the sleepy cafe attendant, then sat down at a table with his breakfast.

As he ate, Hal drew the land outside the window. It was unlike anything he'd seen before. He'd imagined the Arctic as an endless expanse of flat snowscapes under bright blue skies, peopled with polar bears. He now saw that this image was taken from Christmas cartoons and books he'd enjoyed when he was little. It wasn't the truth. The icy reality was more complicated, wild and powerful.

The snow mist, which hung low, reduced visibility, and gave an air of claustrophobia to the landscape. The world outside the window was monochrome, a flat picture made of greys, blacks and whites. So many different whites. *Colour is light,* Hal thought, *but here, there is no direct light, as the sun doesn't rise above the horizon. Snow has the power to suck all the colour from the world.*

The train passed a slate-grey lake. The mist looked like it had been exhaled by the water. Despite the temperature outside being minus eleven, the lake was only frozen around the edges. The unfrozen water was the colour and texture of a seal's skin, all oily grey-greens with dark spots and streaks of silver. Hal thought how he would use his watercolours to add layers of darkness to his drawing.

The door at the far end of the dining car slid open. Glancing up, Hal saw Lars, the architect, entering. As the man passed his table, Hal looked directly at him, smiling. 'Morning,' he said, cheerfully, but the word stuck in his throat, and every muscle in his body went rigid.

The man passing his table was not Lars. He looked so much like him they could be brothers. Like Lars, he was wearing a black polo neck and glasses.

The stranger grunted, but didn't look at Hal.

Realizing his mistake, Hal hunched over his sketchbook, focusing his attention on the page as his heart hammered and his mind whirled. *How can there be two men who look so similar on the same train?* his brain screamed. *Who is this man? Is he the man I drew in the station beside the Dynamic Dozen? Is he the Shadow?*

His first instinct was to gather his things and run back to the compartment to wake up Uncle Nat. However, he knew he shouldn't panic and jump to conclusions. Lars hadn't been the Shadow. Perhaps this man wasn't either. On the other hand, this man hadn't been at the concert last night, and he was breakfasting very early. Surely an assassin would keep a low profile? Especially if he was on a job.

Hal shivered. To be certain, he needed to get a look at the ears of Lars's doppelgänger.

Turning to a clean page, Hal began a new picture, a portrait of the man now selecting his breakfast. He had to be careful, stealing surreptitious glances, but he'd been training for this, drawing fast, taking in information with his eyes and translating it onto the page. As the man paid the cafe attendant, Hal got a feeling of déjà vu. He had drawn this face before. The jawline was familiar, as was the curve of the brow bone. The arms of his spectacles disappeared into his hair, which was short, but covered the tops of his ears.

If I were an assassin and had a distinguishing mark, I'd cover it up too, Hal thought as he continued to draw. And then he stopped, struck by a realization. He *had* drawn this

face more than once. He turned back through the pages of his sketchbook, to the very first drawings he'd done on the aeroplane.

He stared at his picture of the passenger seated in the aisle in front of him, wearing headphones and a denim jacket. If you shaved off the beard and moustache, he looked like the man who was paying for his breakfast right now. He had the same jawline, the same heavy brow, and he remembered a glimpse, between cap and headphones . . . The top part of the man's right ear had been missing! He'd forgotten noticing it on the plane until now.

Hal felt a jolt of fear. He hurriedly turned back to the drawing of the landscape and told himself to be calm. The Shadow didn't know who he was. If he sat quietly drawing the scene out of the window, the man would eventually leave the dining car. Then he could go and alert Uncle Nat. He wished desperately that he hadn't greeted the Shadow. He was an idiot to have drawn attention to himself like that.

From the corner of his eye, he saw that the Shadow had seated himself on the opposite side of the carriage. For Hal, the minutes that passed while the man ate his breakfast felt like the slowest minutes of his life. He could hardly breathe. His hand was shaking as he tried to keep drawing.

He heard the noise of the door behind him opening.

'Ah, Hal, there you are.' Hal's stomach dropped at the sound of Uncle Nat's voice. 'I'm going to get myself a coffee. Do you want anything?'

Hal spun around in his seat. Uncle Nat saw the look of terror on his face. His eyes swept the carriage, pausing for a millisecond as they registered the other person in the room. He smiled easily as he went to the coffee machine.

'I could hear your mother snoring through the compartment wall. Did you come here to escape the noise?'

Hal's mouth opened but he didn't know what to say.

'It was lovely to meet you both last night at the concert. That's one of the things that's so great about travelling by train, don't you think? Meeting people?'

Hal realized that Uncle Nat was protecting him by pretending they'd only just met.

100

'Y-yes,' Hal stammered, taking his lead from his uncle. 'The concert was good, wasn't it?'

'Fabulous.' Uncle Nat paid the attendant for the coffee and sauntered over to Hal's table. 'You drawing again? Such a great skill you have there.'

'Thank you,' Hal said, looking up at his uncle.

Uncle Nat positioned himself with his back to the Shadow, so he was blocking the man's view of Hal. He pulled the sketchbook towards him. 'That's really very good,' he said. 'You've captured the eeriness of the snowy landscape.' Then he dropped his voice and, in a barely audible whisper, said, 'Get up *now*. Go to the compartment. Don't open the door to anyone but me.'

Hal stood up. 'Thanks, Mr Bradshaw.'

Uncle Nat winced as Hal said his real name, and Hal felt panic rising in his chest. If the Shadow didn't know who Uncle Nat was, Hal had just given him away.

'I'd better go and see if Mum's awake yet,' Hal stammered.

'You do that.' Uncle Nat looked stern, but he gave Hal a reassuring smile as he got up from the table. 'I'll see you later.'

CHAPTER FOURTEEN

SHADOW BOXING

Hal stopped walking as soon as the door to the dining car had shut behind him. Not wanting to be visible through the window, he ducked down into the empty luggage-storage space, crouching in the dark. What should he do? He felt sick with fear. He couldn't go back and sit in the compartment, wondering whether Uncle Nat was all right. He had to help him.

There was a noise as the dining-car door opened. Looking up, Hal saw the cafe attendant leave the canteen, walk down the corridor, and go into the toilet.

Uncle Nat was alone in there with the Shadow!

Hal returned to the door, peering through the glass. His uncle was sitting opposite the Shadow at his table. He noticed that the door into the thin room behind the canteen had been left open by the attendant. Acting on instinct, he carefully slid the door aside and crawled furiously to the little room behind the canteen counter.

If I can't see them, Hal told himself, *they can't see me.*

102

Once through the door, Hal kept low, glancing about him. The tiny room was packed with fridges, microwaves and boxes on stainless-steel shelves, alongside trays stacked with ready-made meals and containers stuffed with condiments and cutlery. At the far end of the room, where the attendant operated the till, there was an area under the counter just big enough for him to fit into. Hal grabbed an empty cardboard box, dropping into the vacant space and holding it in front of him so he wouldn't be seen by the attendant.

'Nathaniel Bradshaw.' The Shadow's voice was deep with a French burr. 'I am not surprised to find you on this train.'

'Really?' Uncle Nat replied calmly. 'I am surprised to find you on it. I thought you were dead.'

'Ha! Dying – my favourite kind of disappearing trick.' The Shadow's laugh was dry.

'You've died before?'

'At least three times.'

Uncle Nat fell silent. For the longest time the two men said nothing.

Hal burned to see what was happening. He was wondering whether he might get away with peeping over the counter when he heard the click of the door, and the attendant returning.

'What brings you to the Arctic?' Uncle Nat asked. 'Business or pleasure?'

'I only ever travel for business,' the Shadow replied.

'I see.'

There was a long, uncomfortable silence.

'Don't pretend you don't know why I'm here.' The Shadow

spoke in a tone that Hal thought a cat would use if it could talk to a mouse.

'I genuinely don't,' Uncle Nat said lightly.

'We're both on this train for the same reason.'

'We are? Well, that's a relief. I'm on this train because I'm taking a holiday to see the Northern Lights before Christmas.'

'Don't play games with me.'

'I'm not,' Uncle Nat replied honestly.

'I know you accompanied Dr Sorenson to the Nobel awards.'

'This is about Mortimer?' Uncle Nat sounded immediately guarded. 'But she's not here. I'm travelling alone.'

'Really? You purchased a train ticket in her name. Her compartment is occupied. I've checked. There's a woman in there.'

Hal's heart was in his throat. The Shadow was talking about his mum!

'That's not Mortimer, that's my sister.' Uncle Nat's voice was urgent.

'But you said you were travelling alone.'

Hal could hear the smirk in the Shadow's voice at having caught Uncle Nat in a lie.

'Morti was meant to be travelling with us, but her plans changed at the last minute. I gave my sister her compartment, and you know perfectly well why I didn't tell you about her.'

'Where is Dr Sorenson?'

'I don't know.'

104

'Don't pretend to be a fool, Nathaniel. We both know you aren't one.'

'You'd be amazed at how much I don't know.' Uncle Nat gave a nervous laugh. 'If I had to hazard a guess, I'd say you're here because of Björn Sorenson's Kill Code.'

'But of course.'

'Mortimer doesn't have it. You know that, don't you?'

'My intelligence says otherwise.'

'She destroyed it!'

'So everyone thought . . . until recently.'

'What do you mean?'

'You really don't know, do you?' The Shadow sounded amused.

The cafe attendant shuffled towards Hal, leaning on the counter beside the till, playing a game on his phone. He was oblivious to the intense conversation taking place only a few metres away.

'Morti's in danger?' Uncle Nat paused. 'Am I a target?'

Hal held his breath, waiting for the answer.

'Do you have the Kill Code?'

'No! Of course I don't!'

'Relax.' The Shadow was enjoying Uncle Nat's anger. 'You're not my target.'

'Is there someone on this train with Björn's Kill Code?'

'I'm not going to tell you that,' the Shadow said. 'I'm a professional.'

'The Kill Code is a terrible weapon. Nobody should have it. Mortimer thought she'd destroyed it. If I had it, the first thing I'd do is destroy it.' Uncle Nat had lowered his voice and his tone was urgent. 'Who are you working for?'

'The good guys, of course.' The Shadow gave a great belly laugh. 'I'm not telling you who I'm working for, Nathaniel. I wouldn't, even if it were the British government.'

'But it's not?'

'Stop fishing.' All humour disappeared from the Shadow's voice. 'You might catch a shark.'

'Yes.' Uncle Nat sighed. 'Good point.'

Hal heard the door opening and people entering the dining car. A number of women were talking in Swedish. He thought he recognized Birgitta's warm voice. They passed the counter, to choose their food from the canteen.

'Well, it's been lovely to catch up,' Uncle Nat said politely, 'but I'd better go.'

Hal realized his uncle had been waiting until there were other passengers in the dining car. The Shadow couldn't do anything to him with witnesses present.

'You know I can't let you leave.' The Shadow's voice was low and threatening.

'You said I wasn't your target.'

'You're not, but my identity is a closely guarded secret.'

'One that I have kept for years,' Uncle Nat pointed out, sounding unafraid.

'Because you thought I was dead,' the Shadow growled.

'My article in *The Telegraph* announcing your death did you a favour.'

'Do you know what it feels like to take a hail of bullets

wearing an armoured vest, and then hurl yourself off a cliff into the sea?'

'Perks of the job, eh?' Uncle Nat said. And then Hal heard him say in a cheerful voice, 'Ah, Magnus, my name's Nathaniel. Let me shake you by the hand. I want to congratulate you on last night's concert. It was a delight. I heard you were going to be playing in Kiruna at the St Lucia festival. Is that right?' His voice was moving, and Hal could tell Uncle Nat was walking away from the Shadow.

Hal needed to get out of his hiding place, but the attendant's legs were blocking his exit. There was a queue at the till as members of the Dynamic Dozen lined up to pay for breakfast. He was trapped.

Hal imagined the Shadow getting up and going after Uncle Nat, and felt a burst of terror. He shoved at the cardboard box that was hiding him. It bashed against the attendant's shins, knocking him off balance. He grabbed at the counter as he fell backwards. A tray of sugar packets, UHT milk and stirrers rained down on him.

Hal scrambled out, jumping over the confused and startled man. There was no time to apologize. He needed to help his uncle.

CHAPTER FIFTEEN

IN CASE OF EMERGENCY

Hal threw open the door, pushing past a couple of surprised diners and into the corridor between the carriages. Through the glass in front of him, he saw the Shadow's back. The assassin was making his way calmly through coach, scanning the seats either side of the aisle. Most passengers were asleep or wearing headphones. Hal waited until he'd reached the other end of the carriage before opening the door and hurrying after him. He dropped into the last seat of the carriage and peered through the glass of the next door.

The assassin was walking like a prowling lion, methodically working though the train, pausing to check the toilet and the shower room. Every muscle in the man's thickset body screamed that he was dangerous.

Hal suppressed the jangling alarms going off in his skull. He needed to focus. What should he do?

The Shadow wanted to kill his uncle, but this a passenger train; he couldn't just attack him – there would be witnesses. And his Uncle Nat wasn't an easy man to kill. Uncle Nat knew who he was dealing with. He would have known the Shadow would follow him.

What will Uncle Nat do? Hal asked himself, and found he knew the answer. His uncle would try to deal with the Shadow before he reached their compartments, to protect him and Mum. There was only the next carriage of six-berth compartments in which he could hide, before he reached the one they were staying in.

Hal jumped to his feet, suddenly knowing exactly where Uncle Nat was, and what he was likely to do.

Flashing his head around the corner, Hal glimpsed the Shadow standing outside the first six-berth compartment. Next to it was the empty one that he and Uncle Nat had eaten their dinner in yesterday. Its curtains were drawn, blocking the view inside.

The Shadow approached the compartment door and knocked. The doors slid apart – and a white pillowcase descended over the surprised assassin's head. Hal saw a pair of hands twist it, so the opening closed tightly around the Shadow's neck as he was yanked into the compartment.

Running to the doorway, Hal saw both men on the floor. Uncle Nat was kneeling on the assassin, holding on to the pillowcase with one hand while trying to prevent the man from reaching into his jacket for a weapon. Suddenly the assassin sat bolt upright, correctly guessing where Uncle Nat's head was, headbutting him so hard that Hal heard the crack and gasped.

Uncle Nat fell back. The Shadow scrambled to his knees,

pulling off the pillowcase. In a second, he had his hands around Uncle Nat's neck and was strangling him.

Hal looked on in horror, feeling powerless. He cast his eyes round desperately for something he could use to help, and caught sight of a small red hammer attached to the wall below an emergency sign in Swedish.

Uncle Nat's face grew purple, and his eyes bulged as his hands desperately pulled at the Shadow's wrists.

'NO!' Hal cried out, yanking the hammer from the wall, and hurling it at the Shadow's head with all his might.

Hal's cry made the Shadow turn. The hammer hit him hard on the temple. His eyes snapped wide with shock, then closed as he slumped to the ground unconscious.

Hal pushed the heavy man off Uncle Nat, who was now clutching the lowest bunk, gasping in great gulps of air.

'Are you all right?' Hal asked.

Uncle Nat nodded and said, between breaths, 'You didn't . . . go back . . . to the compartment . . . then?'

Hal shook his head.

'Thanks.'

Hal helped his uncle up to sit on the sofa, then made sure the door and curtains were closed.

'What do we do now?' Hal looked at the Shadow, and was relieved to see he was still breathing.

'Search him. He'll have weapons.' Uncle Nat passed Hal the pillowcase. 'Put them in there.'

Hal started at the Shadow's feet, his body coiled, ready to spring back if the assassin moved. Fearfully he felt around the man's ankles, and found a throwing knife strapped to each one. Patting him down, he discovered three guns, a silencer, a big knife, and a knuckleduster. They all went into the pillowcase. Then Uncle Nat instructed him to go to the door at the end of the carriage, which had a window that slid down, and throw the weapons off the train.

Checking the corridor was clear, Hal ran to the door, an icy blast of air hitting his face as he opened the window. The pillowcase was heavy. It landed in a deep bank of snow, sinking without a trace as the train journeyed on. Hal immediately felt safer.

When he returned, Uncle Nat had laid the Shadow face down on the floor and tied his hands behind his back using the man's shoelaces. He was standing over the unconscious assassin when Hal returned.

'I'm going to need your help,' Uncle Nat said, lifting a complimentary bottle of water from the table. 'I have some questions I want this man to answer.' He opened the bottle and took a swig.

'I have questions too,' Hal said, looking down at the Shadow.

'You'd better hold on to this.' Uncle Nat held out the red

111

hammer. 'If you need to, throw it at him again.'

'OK.' Hal stood with his feet apart, gripping the hammer in anticipation.

Uncle Nat put his knee into the small of the Shadow's back and emptied the bottle of water onto his head to bring him round.

The Shadow spluttered and struggled as he regained consciousness and found he couldn't move.

'Apologies for the ambush,' Uncle Nat said in a soft but steely voice, 'but I was telling you the truth. I really am on holiday, and I'd rather not die on this trip. Nor do I want to harm you, although I appreciate I may have to . . .' He let the sentence hang, unfinished.

The Shadow laughed, turning his head to look at Uncle Nat, but fell silent when he saw Hal. 'Who's the kid?'

'This is my nephew. I'm taking him to see the Northern Lights,' Uncle Nat said. 'I believe you have a policy about children . . . or at least you did.'

'I don't take jobs involving children.' The Shadow stared at Hal. 'Childhood is precious.'

'Don't you hurt my uncle,' Hal growled.

The Shadow crumpled, looking sad. 'That's not a promise I can make.'

'Right,' Uncle Nat said brightly. 'Now we're all introduced, I'd like you to tell me who has the Kill Code.'

'I don't know.'

'But you—'

'Nathaniel, you're mixed up in things you don't understand.'

'What I don't understand is why, all of a sudden, someone thinks Morti has the Kill Code.'

Hal gasped, a thought coming to him in a flash. 'Because, she does!' he exclaimed. 'Or at least, she did, and the only person who could know that is Björn himself.'

'What do you mean?' Uncle Nat frowned.

'Morti said she threw everything that belonged to Björn away, right?'

'Yes.'

'But she must've still loved him because she kept two things that he had given to her: his surname and her wedding ring.'

'You don't know that she kept her wedding ring,' Uncle Nat said. 'She doesn't wear it.'

'Not on her finger, no. But remember that newspaper article that announced Morti was a Nobel Prize winner? We saw it in the museum.' He pulled out his sketchbook and opened it to show his uncle. 'In the picture above the article, Morti was wearing a ring on a chain around her neck. I bet it's her wedding ring.'

'Hmm,' said Uncle Nat. 'A sentimental reminder that she started the journey to find the magic frequency with her husband—'

'Björn must've seen the article!' interrupted Hal. 'The picture is how he knows Morti still has the Kill Code. The article was published in October and that's when all the strange things started to happen.'

'But what's the Kill Code got to do with Morti's wedding ring?' wondered Uncle Nat.

'The Kill Code is engraved on the inside of the ring.' Hal guessed, watching his uncle think this through. 'Mum has the date of her wedding engraved inside her ring. That's a thing people do, isn't it?'

'Your nephew is smart,' the Shadow grunted, sounding impressed.

'Is Morti your target?' Uncle Nat swung back to the shadow.

'No.'

'Is your target after the Kill Code too?' Hal asked, as another idea crashed into his head, disrupting his thoughts.

'Yes.' The Shadow raised an amused eyebrow at Hal's astute question.

'Do they have it?' Uncle Nat asked.

'Possibly.'

'It's a woman!' Hal's heart was beating so fast he thought he might faint. There wasn't one assassin on this train. There were two! 'The woman following us around the Christmas market. The one who tried to steal your wallet. She's after the Kill Code! Uncle Nat! What if she's on this train? What if she thinks Mum is Morti because she's in her compartment?'

'Bev's wedding ring!' Uncle Nat exclaimed. He pushed his knee into the Shadow's back. 'Who is she? Do I know her? Does she have a name?'

'Plenty.' The Shadow laughed as if this were the funniest joke he'd heard in a long time.

Uncle Nat leaped up, away from the laughing assassin. 'Go!' he ordered Hal. 'Get to your mum.'

As Hal yanked the curtains in front of the door aside, he heard a thunderous rumbling, followed by a deafeningly explosive noise. His body jerked as his feet were pulled from under him. Metal screeched as the vacuum brakes slammed on. The train's lights flickered and went out. He heard Uncle Nat shout. He threw his hands out to break his fall but failed to grab on to anything. His head smacked down hard on the side of the bunk and the world went black.

CHAPTER SIXTEEN

AVALANCHE

Hal's head was throbbing. He became aware of Uncle Nat's voice saying his name. He opened his eyes. An icy breeze and dull grey light was coming through the window, which seemed to be directly above him and smashed. He was lying on the compartment door, the bunks reaching up either side of him like theatre flats. He was covered in chunks of safety glass. 'What happened?' Hal groaned.

'I think something hit the train.' His uncle was on his knees beside him. 'We've come off the rails.'

'We've crashed?' Hal tried to sit up. Pieces of glass rolled off him like dice. 'Where's the Shadow?'

'He was lying on the floor when the train tipped. He wasn't thrown.' Uncle Nat looked up. 'He used your emergency hammer and broke the glass.'

'He climbed out of the window?'

'Yes. Can you get up? Are you hurt? We need to get to Bev.' There was urgency in his voice.

'I think I'm all right.' Gripping on to his uncle, Hal stood up, suppressing a dizzying wave of nausea. He looked at the door beneath his feet. 'Are we going to crawl along the corridor?'

'No. It's not safe, and we don't know that we can get into the next carriage.' He grabbed a bunk sheet, and wrapped it around his fist. 'We'll go out of the window.'

The compartment window was about a foot above Uncle Nat's head. He reached up and knocked out the remaining glass, and dropped the sheet. Then he gripped the frame with both fists, using the table-top for leverage, pulling himself up through the casement. His right foot kicked out against the sofa, giving him the boost he needed to push himself up and out of the train. Getting onto his knees, Uncle Nat leaned back through the window.

'Hal, reach up your left arm.' Uncle Nat clamped a hand around Hal's forearm. 'Grab on to me. That's right.' His other hand clamped on to the other side of Hal's arm. 'Can you reach the window frame with your free hand?'

Hal stretched up. His fingers just hooked over it.

'I'm going to count to three. On three you jump, and I'll pull. I want you to grab on to the window with your free hand and pull yourself up too. If your foot finds purchase, push up with your legs.' He smiled encouragingly at Hal. 'Are you ready? One . . . two . . . three!'

The cold air shocked Hal as he was half-hauled, half-climbed, through the window onto the top of the train. Scrambling to his feet, he shoved his hands in his pockets. The sudden drop in temperature cleared his mind and set his body shivering.

From their high vantage point, in the eerie half-light of the Arctic morning, they could see the full extent of the accident.

'Avalanche!' Uncle Nat exclaimed, pointing towards the front of the train. The locomotive was barely visible. It had been pushed off the tracks by a huge snow mass; its nose was on its side, its back end buried, uncoupled from the train. The second and third carriages were at right angles to each other. That's where the Dynamic Dozen's compartments were. The train of carriages zigzagged over the track, but only the locomotive and the carriage Hal was standing on had completely fallen over. The rest were leaning one way or another. He saw a broken rail curling up where the carriages had veered off the track.

'Come on, we'll walk across the top of the train.' Uncle Nat turned his back on the locomotive and set off. 'It'll be quicker. The snow's too deep on the ground.'

'Do you think the driver is all right?' Hal asked, following Uncle Nat. His stomach was as tight as a clenched fist with the fear that they'd find his mum hurt, or worse.

'The locomotive's momentum was stopped by

that great slab of snow. It's fresh and powdery. Hopefully it will have been a relatively soft impact. I'm sure train drivers in the Arctic are trained to deal with avalanches.'

The carriage had separated from the one containing their compartments. Hal could see pipes and wires dangling loose between the buffers.

'We'll have to jump down into the snowdrift,' Uncle Nat said, getting onto all fours, dangling his legs over the side and dropping into the snow. Losing his balance, he fell back, sinking neck deep in the white stuff, but Hal didn't have time to smile. He was already pushing his legs over the edge of the train. The snow was like a cold crashmat, swallowing him up to his waist.

The pair waded to the buffers and hoisted themselves into the carriage. Uncle Nat closed the connecting door behind them, and Hal was relieved to feel the warmth of being back inside. The main lights were off but dim emergency lighting gave off a pale glow. The floor was slanted like an unnerving fairground funhouse. He reached out his hands and pushed against the walls to steady himself as he ran to his mum's compartment. He could hear voices. He strained his ears, hoping to make out his mum's. He pushed open her compartment door. His stomach dropped as he saw the room was empty.

'Mum?' he called out in panic.

'Hal?' His mum's head popped out of baby Alfred's compartment. 'Hal!' Her worried expression bloomed into smiling relief. 'Oh Hal, you're OK! I thought my premonition had come to pass!' She reached out and gathered him into a hug, beaming at Uncle Nat. 'Thank heavens the two of you are safe.'

'We were in the dining car . . .' Uncle Nat didn't finish his sentence.

'Are *you* all right?' Hal asked, studying his mother, looking for any sign that she'd been hurt.

'Me? I'm fine. I was fast asleep. The crash would've thrown me out of the bunk onto the floor if your uncle hadn't told me to put up that elasticated net thing at the side of the bed. Very handy, those things.' She turned to Uncle Nat. 'Do you know what's going on with the train?'

'Avalanche,' Uncle Nat replied.

The word brought Erik and Heidi to the door.

'Avalanche? Oh no!' Erik shook his head. 'We're going to be stuck here for some time then.' He looked at Alfred, who was sleeping in Heidi's arms.

'Mum?' Hal tugged at her hand. 'I bumped my head. It hurts.'

Uncle Nat glanced at Hal, surprised to hear him sounding so young.

'Oh!' His mum immediately looked concerned.

Hal pulled back his hair as he shuffled back into her compartment.

'Ooh, that's quite a bump you've got there.' His mum took his head in her hands and inspected the egg-sized lump that was bulging at the edge of his hairline. 'You might have concussion.'

'I need to sit down,' Hal said, dropping onto her bunk. Uncle Nat followed them in, a mixture of concern and curiosity on his face.

'Follow my finger,' his mum said, moving her index finger from left to right and watching his eyes. 'Do you have a headache?'

'A bit,' Hal said, furtively gesturing to Uncle Nat to close the door. 'Listen, Mum.' He dropped his voice to a whisper as soon as the door was shut. 'I'm fine. It's just a bump on the head. But things are *not* fine on this train.'

'What do you mean?' His mum frowned.

'We have to tell her,' Hal said to Uncle Nat, and he nodded.

'Tell me what?'

'Sit down, Bev,' Uncle Nat said.

She sat beside Hal and took his hand.

'Firstly . . .' Uncle Nat stood before them. 'I want you to focus on the fact that the three of us are together and we're all OK.'

Hal nodded, smiling, trying to look reassuring.

'Oh no. It's bad, isn't it?' His mum's eyes flickered from Nat to him and back. 'I can see it on your faces. What's going on?'

'It's a long story.' Uncle Nat sighed. 'Morti wanted me to go with her to the Nobel awards because she was frightened that someone was following her. It transpires that her ex-husband . . .'

'The evil scientist one?'

'Ha! Yes, him. It seems that he had a code engraved on the inside of her wedding ring and there are powerful people who want that code.'

'What is the code for?'

'A weapon,' Hal said. 'A terrible weapon that could kill a lot of people.'

Hal's mum drew herself up straight. 'I see.' She gripped Hal's hand tightly and looked at Uncle Nat. 'And these people who want that code. Are they on this train?'

Uncle Nat nodded. 'Their employees are.'

'Oh! Wait, was *my* wedding ring taken because I'm here with you, and in Morti's compartment?' she guessed, and Hal was impressed by how quickly she was putting things together.

Uncle Nat nodded again.

'I see.' She glanced at Hal. 'And these employees, are they *dangerous* people?'

Uncle Nat didn't need to nod. His silence spoke volumes.

'Right.' His mum looked at him. 'And you're mixed up in this, I presume?'

Hal nodded.

'And do either of you have Morti's wedding ring?'

'No,' Uncle Nat said firmly.

'Someone's been following me and Uncle Nat ever since Morti disappeared from her hotel in Stockholm.' Hal said.

'Disappeared?' His mum narrowed her eyes as she stared at her brother.

'She left a note,' Uncle Nat spluttered.

'This woman was following us in Stockholm. She tried to pick Uncle Nat's pocket. Katarina saw her.'

'Who's Katarina?' his mum and Uncle Nat asked at the same time.

'The Sámi girl from the Christmas market. She's on the train. We talked last night after the concert. I was going to tell you, but I haven't had a chance.'

'The person following you is a woman?' Bev asked.

'One of them is,' Hal said.

'*One of them?*'

'We don't know how many people are after that code,' Uncle Nat admitted.

'But you don't have the code?'

'No, I told you.'

'Let me get this straight. You're telling me that we're stranded in the Arctic on a derailed train that's been hit by an avalanche, and there's at least one person on this train who

123

thinks we've got some sort of a deadly code that they've been *employed* to get?'

'Yes,' Uncle Nat muttered. 'That's about the size of it.'

'Well then, you'd better tell me precisely what you intend to do about it.' Hal's mum folded her arms across her chest and glared at both of them.

CHAPTER SEVENTEEN

BLOODLINE

'First, we're getting out of this compartment,' Uncle Nat said, grabbing the carrier bags Hal's mum was using for her luggage. 'We're sitting ducks in here. Get your stuff and let's go.'

Hal helped his mum collect the loose items from her bunk and beside the sink, and they followed Uncle Nat into his compartment. Once they were inside, he locked the door.

Hal looked at the mess on the floor. His art supplies and pyjamas had tumbled from his bunk, along with Uncle Nat's toiletries which had fallen from the sink. Sitting down on the sofa, he opened his sketchbook and turned to the picture he'd drawn at the Christmas market. It was impossible to know what the mysterious pickpocket looked like because of her headscarf and sunglasses.

'Bev?' Uncle Nat sat down between her and Hal. 'We know who one of the people after the ring is.'

'But he said he wasn't after the ring . . .'

Uncle Nat shot Hal a look, but it was too late. The

125

words were out of his mouth.

'Hal has *met* this man?' His mother's words sounded like an accusation. She was looking at Uncle Nat without blinking.

Uncle Nat's face stiffened, and Hal wondered what he was going to say.

'Bev, this morning I was threatened by a man I knew a long time ago. Hal came to my aid. He was brave and I might not be standing here right now if he hadn't. I'm not going to lie to you. The people we're dealing with are dangerous.'

Hal held up his drawing. 'This is the woman who was following us in Stockholm.'

His mum peered at it. 'But she could be anyone. She could be me. If she's on this train, how are we going to know what she looks like?'

'We won't,' Uncle Nat said. 'We need to be wary of everyone. You've obviously met her, Bev. She took the wedding ring right off your hand last night.'

His mum clutched her empty ring finger.

'Do you remember talking to anyone last night?' Hal asked.

'Yes! I talked to everyone. I shook hands with every member of the Dynamic Dozen, I met Lars . . . he is such a sweet man. Do you know, immediately after the train crashed, he came running to my compartment to check that I was all right, even though he was wounded.' She touched her temple to show where. 'He had a nasty bruise.'

Hal and Uncle Nat exchanged an alarmed look.

'What did he say?' Uncle Nat asked.

'He knocked on the door and asked if I was all right. I was

126

frightened. He calmed me down, and then offered to pick up all of my things that had fallen out of the two bags. I went to your compartment to check on you, but you didn't answer. I was worried. Lars told me not to worry about you two, saying that he'd seen you in the dining car.'

Hal felt sick. The man who'd pretended to help his mum had been the Shadow. He'd used the crash as an excuse to search her compartment. He must've lied about not being after the ring.

'You shouldn't have opened your door to him, Bev,' Uncle Nat said. 'You don't know who anyone is.'

'Well excuse me for not knowing I should be suspicious!' Bev snapped. 'Lars is nice. You seemed to like him last night.'

'The man who helped you wasn't Lars, Mum,' Hal said. 'He was the man who threatened Uncle Nat. People call him the Shadow. He looks a lot like Lars.'

'But . . .' His mum frowned. She looked down as she recalled the man helping her. 'I thought it was him.'

'If you needed help, you should have called for Inga, the carriage attendant,' Uncle Nat said.

'Inga?' His mum's puzzled expression deepened. 'But there isn't a carriage attendant, Nat. The only attendant on the train is Sven, the young man in the cafe. He was grumbling about it last night.'

Hal's heart stopped. He was already flicking forward to the page where he'd drawn Inga. He flipped backwards and forwards between the Christmas market picture and the picture of Inga. *Were they the same woman?*

127

Uncle Nat's mouth was open, his eyes darting from left to right. He looked at Hal. 'She assumed we were a party of three when there were only the two of us in the compartment, do you remember?'

'She was looking for Morti!' Hal exclaimed. 'At least we have a better picture of her.' He held up the sketch.

'I wish it wasn't from above,' said Uncle Nat, staring at the page. 'We need a good front-on image. Bev, have you seen this woman?' He leaned back so she could look at the picture. 'She could be the person who took your ring.'

His mum took her time, then shook her head. 'I don't think I have. Sorry.'

'What happened after the Shadow left you?' Uncle Nat asked.

'I could hear little baby Alfred crying so I knocked on their compartment door to see if he was all right. Lars – I mean, the Shadow – said he needed to get back to his own compartment and that I should stay with them until help came. He said there was safety in numbers.'

'That's good advice,' Uncle Nat said begrudgingly.

'Then Heidi came back from the bathroom. She'd hurt her arm in the crash and was bleeding. I offered to take a look at it, and then you two came along.'

Hal was staring down at his picture of the Dynamic Dozen. 'You don't think our mysterious woman is in the orchestra, do you? I mean, why did the Shadow attach himself to this group? Do you think he was following her?'

Uncle Nat and his mum looked at the picture.

'It's one thing to pretend to be a train attendant. Anyone can do that,' his mum said. 'But playing a musical instrument to such a high level takes a lifetime.'

'We can't rule anyone out,' Uncle Nat said. 'From now on, we do not trust anyone on this train. Got that?'

Hal nodded along with his mum, although there was one person he knew he *could* trust on the train, who'd seen the woman in the Christmas market: Katarina.

'We'd better pack our things,' Uncle Nat said. 'They'll be moving everyone off the train. It isn't going anywhere. They'll probably put us on a coach as soon as they can get one here. We should go and sit in the dining car until then. We need to be among other people. It'll be safer.'

'Wait, aren't we going to try and find this woman?' Hal pointed at Inga. 'She took Mum's wedding ring. She's obviously after that code.'

'No! We need to stay away from her. She's dangerous,' Uncle Nat insisted, and Bev agreed. 'What I'd like to know –' he exhaled sharply – 'is where that ruddy Kill Code is, so I can destroy it once and for all. We think it's engraved inside Morti's wedding ring, but where *is* her wedding ring?'

Hal's hands shot to his temples as an image flew into his head, his sketchbook dropping to the floor. 'Oh! I know where it is!' he exclaimed, looking at Uncle Nat in horror. 'We *do* have it!'

CHAPTER EIGHTEEN

RINGSIDE

'Morti said the Kill Code was a series of frequencies, which must mean it's a list of numbers.' Hal looked at Uncle Nat for confirmation, and he nodded. 'Mum, you've got numbers engraved on the inside of your wedding ring.'

'Yes, but they refer to dates, not a code that can kill people.'

'Is it only the date of your wedding?' Uncle Nat asked.

'No, I added the date of Hal's birth and later Ellie's.'

'There are nine numbers inside your wedding ring?' Uncle Nat seemed surprised.

'That may be why the thief thought it was the Kill Code,' Hal said. 'Which is good, because it means they don't know exactly where the real ring with the Kill Code is.'

'But you do?' Uncle Nat asked.

'How is that possible?' his mum asked. 'We don't have Morti's wedding ring.'

'I think we do,' said Hal, leafing through the pages of

his sketchbook. 'When we met in Stockholm, Morti wasn't wearing the ring on a necklace, which means that since the Nobel Prize announcement she either took it off or put it somewhere different. It can't have been in her jewellery box, because it would've been taken in the burglary, so I think she took it off the necklace and put it somewhere else.'

'But where?' Uncle Nat asked.

Hal found the page he was looking for and held it up. 'Her keyring.' He pointed to his drawing of the keys Morti had given them to her cabin in Kiruna. His mum and uncle leaned in to look. 'There!' He pointed to the decorative ring attached to the leather fob. 'I noticed something was inscribed inside, but it meant nothing to me, so I've just done scribbles. What if it's the Kill Code?' He looked at Uncle Nat. 'And we've been carrying it with us since Stockholm.'

'Let's see, shall we?' Uncle Nat turned to Hal's mum. 'Bev, you'd better give me those keys. It's not safe for you to have them.'

Grabbing her coat and unzipping the pocket, Hal's mum rooted around, then frowned and unzipped the other pocket. 'I could have sworn I put the keys in here.'

'You did, I saw you.' A cold, sinking feeling dragged at Hal's stomach.

His mum looked alarmed. 'They're gone.'

'Did you take them out?' Uncle Nat said.

'No, I hung the coat on the back of my compartment door when I moved my stuff and it's stayed there till now.'

'The Shadow!' Hal hissed.

Uncle Nat nodded. 'He must have taken the keys when he was in your compartment after the crash.'

'What should we do?' Hal's mum asked.

'Do?' Uncle Nat frowned.

'You're not going to let this Shadow person get away with that Kill Code, are you?' His mum looked horrified. 'People will die!'

'I . . . er . . .' Uncle Nat glanced at Hal.

'Mum's right.' Hal nodded. 'We have to get those keys back.'

'We have to stop him,' she insisted.

'These are dangerous people . . .' Uncle Nat faltered in the face of his sister and nephew's determined expressions. 'Fine. We'll try. But, if we're going to get that ring back, you have to do as I tell you. OK?'

They nodded.

'Do you know where the Shadow's compartment is?' Hal asked.

'No. Although we can rule out the six-berth compartments. He won't be sharing.'

Hal flicked through his sketchbook to the train diagram he'd drawn. 'He isn't in the first carriage – that's full of the Dynamic Dozen – which means he's either in the second carriage, this carriage or the last carriage in the train.'

'He isn't in this carriage,' Uncle Nat said. 'We would have seen him yesterday.'

'So, carriage two or carriage nine.'

'Carriage nine is next door,' Hal's mum said. 'Should we check that one first?'

'Yes, but before we do, Bev, you need to understand that this man is a professional killer. He has no scruples and is a skilled liar. If you have to hit him, make sure you hit him as hard as you can.'

'Got it.' Hal's mum nodded. 'If he threatens any of us, I'll knee him in the nuts.'

Hal suppressed a smile at Uncle Nat's alarmed expression.

As they left the compartment, Hal saw that the other doors were all open. The rooms had been vacated. Everyone had had the same idea – to get to the coach and dining cars where there was food and other passengers. He shivered. It was creepy: the grey half-light filtering through the windows, the pale emergency lights near the floor, the tilt of the carriage.

'Where are we?' Hal asked, looking out the window. 'Do you know?'

'Not exactly,' Uncle Nat replied. 'Somewhere between Boden and Kiruna. Near Gällivare I think.'

The growl of a pair of motors came from outside the train. Two bright red snowmobiles were racing along the trackside towards the wreckage of the engine, their headlights cutting through the gloom, beaming onto the snow. To Hal's surprise and delight, behind them ran a reindeer pulling a sledge. His face was so close to the window that his breath misted the glass. He wiped the condensation off with his sleeve. 'Who are they? Are they from the train company?'

'They look like Sámi people,' Uncle Nat said, and Hal thought of Katarina and her aunt.

'C'mon.' Hal's mum waved them forward. 'We need to get those keys back.' Hal could tell she felt responsible for losing them.

The three of them cautiously made their way to the adjoining door and peered into carriage nine.

'It looks empty,' Hal whispered.

'Let's not make assumptions,' Uncle Nat replied.

The first three compartments had been vacated; their doors were wide open. The door of the fourth was closed. Uncle Nat glanced at them, checking they were prepared. Hal nodded, clenching his fists in readiness as his uncle turned the handle and pushed the door.

The three of them drew breath at the sight that greeted them. The compartment had been smashed up. The mirror above the sink was cracked. The top bunk hung at an angle. Bedding was on the floor and, trussed up like a chicken, tied to the bunk ladder, was the Shadow. A piece of gaffer tape covered his mouth.

'Lars!' Hal's mum exclaimed.

'That's not Lars,' Hal told her.

His mum winced as Uncle Nat ripped the tape off.

'We must stop meeting like this,' Uncle Nat said.

'Suits me,' the Shadow grunted.

'Where are the keys?' Hal's mum demanded.

'Keys?' The Shadow looked at her. 'What keys?'

'Let me handle this, Bev,' Uncle Nat said, stepping into the Shadow's eyeline.

Hal opened a suitcase that was sitting on the bottom bunk. 'Look!' He grabbed Uncle Nat's arm, pulling out a dark wig with a blunt fringe and ponytail. 'It's the waitress from the hotel bar in Stockholm!' He opened his sketchbook and showed the picture to his mum. 'That must have been when

she stole Uncle Nat's phone and room key.' Taking out his pen, Hal set about drawing the room on a clean page.

'This isn't your compartment, is it?' Uncle Nat said to the Shadow.

The Shadow stared belligerently at him.

Hal was emptying the suitcase onto the bunk, item by item. 'Mum!' Hal held up a gold band.

'My wedding ring!' His mum put it straight onto her finger and beamed at Hal.

'There are four different phones in here. Uncle Nat, is this yours?'

'If there are a hundred missed calls from your mother, then it's my phone.'

'I can't tell. It's got no battery.'

'Of course it's my phone. Who else has an old analogue phone?'

Hal tied a leopard-print scarf round his head and put on a pair of oversized sunglasses. He held up a red waistcoat. 'She was the waitress, the pickpocket, and the attendant, Inga.'

'Who is she?' Uncle Nat asked the Shadow.

The Shadow shrugged. 'Are you going to untie me?'

'Probably not,' Uncle Nat replied, taking the large white envelope Hal handed to him. It contained photographs. Most were of Mortimer, but the last one was of him with Hal getting aboard the Arlanda Express. Uncle Nat's eyebrows drew together and he turned the kind of pale that he only went when he was very, very angry. His lips pressed together in a thin determined line. '*Who is she?*' His voice was steely.

'Don't know her name,' the Shadow replied.

'She bested you?'

The Shadow's head dropped a little.

'Who is she?'

'I told you . . .'

'You know something, or you wouldn't be strapped to a ladder. You don't know a lot or you'd be dead.'

'She's the Chameleon,' he replied in a gritty whisper.

'The Chameleon?' Uncle Nat looked astonished. 'I thought she was a myth.'

'And you thought that I was dead.' The Shadow gave Uncle Nat a sardonic smile. 'I bet you wish I were, now. Right?'

'Does she have the Kill Code?' Uncle Nat asked.

'I don't know. Is it . . .' The Shadow looked at Hal's mum. '. . . on the keys?'

Hal's mum turned away, busying herself by sorting through the disguises on the bunk.

'He doesn't have it,' Hal said to Uncle Nat. 'Someone else must have broken into our compartment. Either that or she took it off him.'

'She didn't take anything off me,' the Shadow snapped.

'Then how did she get into Mum's compartment?' Hal wondered.

'She could have gone in dressed as Inga,' Uncle Nat said. 'Maybe during last night's concert? No one would have thought it suspicious.'

'But how did she know where –' he glanced at the Shadow – '*it* was?'

'We have to find her!' Uncle Nat said, shaking his head.

'Nat, we have no way of knowing what this woman looks like,' Hal's mum said. 'These are the disguises she's finished with. We don't know which one she's wearing right now.'

Hal picked up a beanie from the case, suddenly remembering the girl from Kungsträdgården, and shivered.

'She's gone,' the Shadow said. 'You'll never find her.'

'Where can she go?' Uncle Nat said. 'We're stuck in the middle of nowhere, in the snow, in the dark.'

'Assassins like the dark.' The Shadow laughed, and it unnerved Hal.

'Why aren't you dead?' Hal asked the bound man, narrowing his eyes, wondering if the two assassins could be working together. 'She could've killed you, but she didn't.'

'She might have, but I suspect she knew you'd be searching for her. I'm a good old-fashioned delaying tactic. The more time you spend here talking to me, the further away she gets,' the Shadow answered flatly. 'She has the Kill Code. Her priority now is to meet her contact and deliver it.'

'We need to find out if she's still on the train,' Hal said to Uncle Nat. 'I'm going to go to the end of the carriage and see if there are any tracks in the snow. She may have left by the end door.'

But when Hal got there, the door was shut and the snow outside was a blemish-free expanse of white. He turned to look towards the front of the train and saw the snowmobiles and sleigh were parked a little back from the capsized engine. Two figures in blue, Katarina and her aunt, were approaching the three men standing by the vehicles. Katarina hugged the man who'd been driving the reindeer. He was older than the other two, who were greeting Katarina's aunt affectionately.

A thought struck Hal. If the Chameleon hadn't left the train, then she must have passed by their cabin while they were all inside, and gone on to the dining car like the other passengers. Hal went back to the compartment, and as he entered saw what Uncle Nat could not. Behind his back, the Shadow had a knife protruding from his sleeve, and was working the blade against the ropes. Several were already cut. He was only pretending to be trussed up!

'Uncle Nat!' Hal cried out, just as the Shadow swung his arm, the knife blade between his fingers.

Uncle Nat fell back, knocking Bev onto the bunk. The Shadow bent down, using the knife to saw through the ropes holding his ankles. Uncle Nat was back on his feet and hit the assassin with a right uppercut. The contact made a horrible noise. The Shadow drew back his arm and elbowed Uncle Nat in the stomach.

'What are you doing?' Uncle Nat gasped as he doubled over.

'My job,' the Shadow said in a bone-chilling voice as he rushed towards the door. Hal stumbled backwards into the corridor, as the assassin bounded away, up the train.

'Get after him,' Uncle Nat wheezed as Hal's mum put her arms around him. 'He knows who she is! He knows where the keys are!'

CHAPTER NINETEEN

ICE-CAPADES

Hal and his mum ran down the corridor, past their compartment, where their packed bags were waiting, to the next connecting door. They stopped abruptly.

'We don't know if the Shadow carried on up the train or left it, climbing out into the snow,' Hal said. He peered through the gap between the disconnected carriages. It was the way that he and Uncle Nat had come in. They'd churned up the snow, so it was impossible to tell if someone else had gone that way.

Uncle Nat came hurrying up behind them, his arm across his stomach. 'What's wrong?'

'He could have gone up the train or out into the snow,' Hal's mum explained.

'We'll split up,' Uncle Nat said.

'Mum and I will go out in the snow,' Hal volunteered.

'OK, but if you see the Shadow, I want you to steer clear, just watch him. His going after the Chameleon could be to our advantage.'

They nodded, wishing him luck as he jumped to the overturned carriage and disappeared inside.

'I'll go and get our coats,' Hal said to his mum, dashing away. He was back a couple of minutes later with an armful of hats, gloves, scarves and coats.

All wrapped up, Hal and his mum dropped into the snow, walking away from the wreck, so that they had a clear view of the whole train all the way to the buried locomotive.

It was a shocking sight. Hal found it upsetting to see a train off the tracks, its carriages all at odd angles to one another.

'I hope no one was hurt,' Hal's mum said as they trudged towards where the avalanche had hit.

'I don't see any sign of the Shadow,' Hal said, straining his eyes in the dim light. 'Do you think we should go back inside the train and help Uncle Nat?'

'Your uncle can take care of himself. Look – everyone is gathered in the lounge and dining cars.' She pointed, and Hal could see the carriages were crowded with silhouettes. 'He should be safe.'

As they approached the site of the avalanche, Hal realized with a jolt that the accident could have been a lot worse. The locomotive, which was tipped on its side in a bank of snow to the right of the tracks, had crashed into a huge wall of snow that had swept down the hillside, pushing a silver Volvo and several trees with it. The smashed-up silver bonnet was sticking out of the snow. A group of people, some train personnel and three Sámi men were standing with their hands on their hips, pointing and talking Swedish.

'I'll find out what's going on with the crash, shall I?' Hal's mum said, striding towards the group. 'The Shadow must still be on the train and they may have a plan to get us all out of here.'

Hal saw Katarina, sitting in the sledge, alone and looking sulky. 'Hi,' he said, approaching her, but staring at the reindeer.

'*Hej, hej,*' she replied and nodded to the train. 'What a mess, eh?'

'It looks worse from out here.'

'Were you hurt?' She tipped her head, studying his face.

'Bump on the head.' He lifted his fringe. 'You?'

'No. I was sleeping. It woke me up.' Katarina snorted with amusement as Hal continued to stare at the reindeer. 'You can pat him if you want to.'

'Oh! No. Thanks.' Hal felt himself blush. 'But I would like to draw him.'

'You can draw him.'

Hal took out his sketchbook and pen and pulled off his right glove. 'What's his name?'

'Girjak.'

'What does Girjak mean?' Hal asked, as he drew the reindeer's branching antlers.

'It means . . . how would you say it . . . *common.*'

Hal blinked at this. He looked into the reindeer's big brown eyes and thought how wonderful it would be to think a beautiful beast like this was common. His hand had to move fast, his skin was tingling and stiffening from the icy

temperature. 'Are they your family?' He pointed his pen at the
Sámi men.

'My uncle and cousins. They were on the way to the
Winter Market in Jokkmokk. My aunt called them and told
them about the crash. The cafe attendant said that the driver
had radioed to Kiruna and coaches were coming to transport
passengers off the train, but it could take a few hours.'

Hal stared at the men beside the locomotive. 'I hope the
driver is OK.'

'The cafe attendant said there were no serious injuries.'

'That's my mum coming towards us,' Hal said.

'I saw her last night at the concert.'

'Hi, I'm Beverly,' his mum said, smiling. 'You must be Katarina. Hal's told me all about you.'

Hal's mouth dropped open at this statement, and Katarina looked at him with a raised eyebrow. 'I didn't, I mean, I said that . . .'

Katarina chuckled.

'Hal says you are travelling with your aunt?'

'Åsa is my aunt.' Katarina pointed. 'Niillas, my pig-headed cousin, is next to her.' She looked searchingly into the gaggle of people. 'And somewhere in there is my uncle and my other cousin. They have come to take us home from here.'

'Why do you call your cousin pig-headed?' Hal's mum asked.

'He won't let me drive home on the snowmobile.' Katarina scowled. 'He says I must sit in the sledge because I'm a little girl.' She tutted. 'I am fourteen!'

'Finished.' Hal shook out his hand, which was freezing, and put his glove back on before showing Katarina his picture.

'Huh! It's good.' She nodded.

'Mum, is it all right if I go over there, just for five minutes?' Hal pointed his pen. 'I want to draw the derailed train.'

His mum nodded, and as Hal walked away, he heard her asking Katarina about the market in Jokkmokk. Katarina said that her uncle carved wooden pots and was going to sell them there.

Wading through the snow, Hal turned regularly until he was happy with his position and his view of the train. He was going to have to be quick. His hand was half frozen from drawing the reindeer.

While he was speedily drawing the mess of lines that made up the derailed train, Hal heard a cry, followed by the chainsaw rev of an engine. He looked up, hearing angry shouts. Two men were on the ground, in the snow. One of the snowmobiles was zooming away up the snowy incline. A slight figure dressed in black was riding it. Hal tried to run back towards the train but the deep snow dragged at his legs, slowing him down. He had a horrible feeling the Chameleon was on that snowmobile, escaping with the Kill Code.

The man that Katarina had called Niillas jumped onto the other snowmobile to give chase. The engine revved. He was turning in the snow, moving to go after the stolen vehicle, when, from behind a tree, a figure Hal recognized came at him, violently shoving him off his seat. Niillas rolled into the snow as the Shadow threw his leg over, and zoomed off after the first bike.

Hal sprinted back to Katarina, who was watching the scene with wide-eyed shock.

'We can't let them get away,' Hal gasped.

'Get in,' Katarina said, gathering the reindeer's reins.

'Hal?' His mum spun around as he jumped onto the sledge. 'Wait for me!'

'*Yah!*' Katarina called out, slapping the reins against Girjak's sides.

As they pulled away, Beverly Beck grabbed the side of the sledge, and jumped aboard.

CHAPTER TWENTY

COLD PURSUIT

Katarina's uncle shouted something at her as they flew past the group of men.

'Uncle's wooden carvings,' Katarina called to Hal, nodding at the large sack taking up the back seat. 'Put them out of the sledge.'

Hal and his mum lifted the sack between them and dropped it over the side into the soft snow, and immediately the sledge picked up speed. Behind them Hal saw Uncle Nat running out from behind the train, looking round in desperation for some way to follow them, but there were no vehicles left.

It was surprising how fast the reindeer could run. The bowed runners of the sledge hared over the snow. It would never achieve the speed of a snowmobile, but the tracks of the vehicles were clear in the snow in front of them and Katarina was careful about the route she directed Girjak to take, keeping a practised eye on the path ahead.

'Look at these marks.' She pointed ahead to a mass of

disturbed snow, slowing the sledge as they passed. 'They are driving too fast. Someone has come off here but got back on again.'

Hal wondered: had the Shadow been knocked off his snowmobile, or the Chameleon? He fancied he could hear the vehicles ahead of them, but all he could see were tracks.

'Are you going to tell me what is going on?' Katarina asked. 'Who are they?'

'They are . . . assassins,' Hal replied, unable to think of a better way of putting it. The shocked expression on Katarina's face almost made him smile. 'One of them is the woman who was following us around the Christmas market.'

'Then shouldn't we be going in the other direction?' she asked. 'I like my life better than a snowbike.'

'One of them has stolen something very dangerous,' Hal's mum explained. 'If it falls into the wrong hands, it can be made into a weapon that could kill many, many, people.'

'But if they've got a dangerous weapon . . .'

'They don't,' Hal said. 'They have a code, a string of numbers, frequencies, that combined can make a sound that can kill.'

'Sound that can kill?' Hal's mum looked horrified. 'You never told me that.'

'Where did this code come from?' Katarina asked.

'A scientist discovered the Kill Code when they were working on a cure for cancer.'

'Is the scientist on the train?' Katarina looked intrigued.

'No, the scientist gave the code to my Uncle Nat without

him realizing that's what she was doing. The woman you saw following us around the Christmas market has been trying to get it ever since.'

'And she has it now?' Katarina asked.

'I think so,' Hal replied. 'The man following her wants the code too. We can't let either of them get it. We must get those keys back.'

'Keys?'

'The code is on a key ring,' Hal's mum said. 'And it was stolen from my coat pocket.' She paused, a thought occurring to her that made her draw breath. 'Oh! Hal, I know who stole the keys. It was Heidi!'

'Heidi? But she's Erik's . . .' He'd been going to say 'wife', but he stopped himself. He'd been in Erik's compartment. There'd been no evidence of a woman there. When had they first met Heidi? It had been at the concert. 'She took your wedding ring?'

'Yes! I thought she was little Alfred's mother, but I realize now, she never said that, and though she flirted with Erik, I never saw them touch.' His mother's eyes were wide. 'And then last night, she came into my compartment for a natter before bed. She tried my coat on. She said she liked it. She put her hands in the pockets and looked in the mirror. That's when she must have taken the keys!'

Hal's mouth had gone dry. His mum had been in a compartment with an assassin. She'd been in terrible danger while he'd been asleep next door. He hadn't even known. He took her hand. Suddenly, having adventures

149

didn't feel like fun. He wished he was back at home, in Crewe, with Bailey the dog on his bed.

'It's OK,' she reassured him, squeezing his hand. 'I'm OK.'

'You said Heidi came back from the bathroom after hurting her arm in the crash, but I'll bet that injury was from her fight with the Shadow.'

'I thought we were becoming friends,' his mum said, sounding a little sad. 'She gave me her address so that I could write to her.'

Hal gritted his teeth, feeling a seething anger building in his stomach. Who was this woman? She was a waitress, a pickpocket, a girl in a beanie, a train attendant, and Heidi! She had bested the Shadow in a fight. She had worked out where the Kill Code was, and stolen it, all without them ever realizing that she was constantly watching them. He had thought he was a good detective, but he'd never encountered a person like the Chameleon before. And for the first time since he'd started having adventures with his uncle, he found he was truly afraid.

They all heard the sickening sound of a weapon being fired and birds shot up out of the snow-laden trees around them. Katarina slowed the sledge. The sound came again and again. Then silence. Hal strained his ears listening for the distant buzz of the snowmobiles, but he couldn't hear them any more.

'Who is shooting at who?' Katarina asked quietly.

'They could both be shooting at each other,' Hal replied.

Katarina pulled the sledge to a stop.

'If you want to go back to the train, Katarina—' his mum said.

'No.' Katarina cut her off. 'I do not want a sound in the world that kills. There is too much killing already.' She pulled a small pair of binoculars from a suede bag that hung diagonally across her chest; she focused them and pointed. 'There is something out there, on the ice.'

Hal stared out at the vast expanse of white in front of them and realized it had to be a frozen lake. There were no rocks, and nothing was growing on it. No trees. No shrubs or plants. How easy it would be to accidentally run out across it, unaware of the danger of the ice cracking and the deadly cold water beneath. He'd always thought of snow as fun, as the only kind of weather to turn the world into a playground, but out here in the Arctic, he could see how dangerous it was. The landscape that he'd once seen as magical was infused with menace. 'What can you see?'

'Out there on the lake.' Katarina handed him the binoculars.

Looking through the lenses, Hal gasped as he saw, in the middle of the plain of ice, a dark figure lying in a pool of blood.

'Let me see.' His mum took the binoculars. 'Oh! Someone is injured, but I can't see who!'

Katarina looked at Hal. 'Is this one of your assassins?'

Hal nodded.

'They'll bleed to death out there,' his mum said, looking distressed. 'We have to help them.'

'It is not wise to walk on the ice,' Katarina said. 'It is too early in the season.'

'But if we don't help, they'll die!' Hal's mum exclaimed.

'And if we do help, *we* may die,' Katarina replied calmly.

'Before we do anything,' Hal said, 'we need to be sure the other assassin has gone. Anyone walking onto the ice is a sitting duck.'

His mum looked surprised. It hadn't occurred to her that helping might make them a target.

'Anyone who walks on that ice will be a drowning human,' Katarina muttered, but she pointed to the snowmobile tracks and flicked the reins so that Girjak trotted forward, following them down through the trees to the edge of the frozen water.

Hal's mum stared across the lake through the binoculars, worry lines creasing her brow. Hal took out his sketchbook and a pen.

The tracks of both snowmobiles curved. Katarina halted the sledge again. They could see where the two vehicles had chased each other. Then Hal saw a red machine on its side across the lake, several metres from the injured person. It was a snowmobile. There must have been a fight.

'The tracks of the other snowmobile go that way.' Katarina pointed to a trail leading away from the ice. 'The other snow rider is gone, heading towards Kiruna.' She looked at Hal. 'What do we do now?'

'Do you think we can reach the person on the ice?' Hal's mum asked.

'Maybe.' Katarina narrowed her eyes. 'They're a long way out.' Stepping from the sledge, she rummaged under the animal hides that covered the wooden seat and pulled out a long length of coiled rope which she pulled over her head, wearing it diagonally across her body. 'I will go and see.' She fixed Hal's mum with a serious stare. 'You must both stay here with Girjak. My people are the Sámi. We know snow and ice. We can read it. You cannot.'

'Will the ice hold your weight?' Hal asked.

'I am the lightest of the three of us.' She shrugged. 'We will see.'

'Be careful,' Hal's mum said, and Katarina nodded. Then she turned and, with a calm and steady gait, walked out onto the ice.

Hal found he was holding his breath. He opened his sketchbook and started to draw the lake.

His mother had the binoculars trained on the prone figure. 'They could already be dead, I can see blood on the ice,' she said in a hushed voice. 'Oh, they moved!'

'What're they doing?' Hal asked, wishing he had the binoculars

'I think they've seen Katarina. They're trying to move.'

'NO!' they heard a man's voice shout. 'STAY BACK!'

'It's the Shadow!' Hal said under his breath. 'The Chameleon shot him!'

Katarina had paused.

'Can I see?' Hal held out his hand for the binoculars. 'What's Katarina doing?'

154

'She seems to be studying the ice.' His mum handed the binoculars over.

'She's got down on her hands and knees,' Hal said, moving the dial so that Katarina came into focus. 'She's pushing at the ice with her hands. Now she's moving forward. Oh!' he exclaimed, as Katarina pushed down on the ice and it sank into the water. A metre away, the other end of the sheet lifted. 'The ice is broken!' Hal clambered up onto the back of the sledge to get a better view. Katarina was pushing all around her, trying to find a way across the broken surface of the ice to the wounded man. She was about five metres away from him. He was signalling for her to go back and leave him, but she was paying him no attention. Finding her feet, she slowly stood up and lifted the coil of rope off. She made a loop at the end of it, deftly tying a knot, and started to swing it around her head.

'What's she doing?' Hal's mum said.

'I think she's going to try and lasso him!' Hal was glued to the binoculars.

Katarina's lasso flew up and out across the broken ice, landing a foot from the Shadow. He grabbed at it. She shouted something Hal couldn't hear and was miming for him to put it over his head and get it under his armpits. Once he had done as she instructed, Katarina turned around, marching with purpose back towards the sledge, feeding out the rope. It ran out three metres from the edge of the frozen lake.

'Get out of the sledge,' she commanded as she approached.

Hal and his mum did as they were told. Katarina took

Girjak's wooden yoke and guided him to the lake side, reversing the sledge onto the ice until it reached the rope. She tied the rope to the back of the sledge, turned to the Shadow and cried, 'HOLD ON!'

CHAPTER TWENTY-ONE

RESCUE REINDEER

'Take Girjak's harness,' Katarina called to Hal, 'and walk forward slowly. He will come with you.'

Hal hesitantly moved onto the ice, approaching the reindeer, aware that with one angry jerk of his head Girjak could gore him with an antler. But the reindeer looked at him with docile eyes and didn't flinch when Hal took hold of the harness. Slowly and steadily, Hal walked forwards and Girjak walked with him, pulling the sledge back towards the snowy shore and solid land. Katarina stayed where she was, watching as the Shadow was slowly pulled across the surface of the frozen lake towards her. He lay down flat, spreading his bodyweight across the ice, making himself rigid, as the ice sheets below him bobbed and buckled.

Hal focused all his attention on keeping the reindeer moving forward. He expected to hear the injured assassin cry out in pain at some bump or jolt, but the man was silent.

'It's working,' his mum said, and Hal looked back over his shoulder to see the wounded man being slowly dragged across the ice, leaving a bloody trail behind him.

Katarina guided the rope, cautiously approaching the Shadow as he slid towards her. Girjak and the sledge were now back on land and proceeding a little faster. Hal's mum went to the edge of the frozen lake, as close to the brave girl as she could get without adding her weight to the ice.

'You will do as I say,' Katarina commanded. 'We will drag you on to the snow.'

The Shadow moved his head to show he understood.

Slowly she and Girjak dragged the bleeding man, until he was lying safely in the soft white powder by the side of the lake.

Katarina patted the reindeer, producing a handful of what looked like pale moss from her pocket and feeding it to him.

'What's that?' Hal asked.

'Lichen,' Katarina replied. 'Reindeer food.'

The three of them drew together, standing a metre from the Shadow, looking down at him. He opened his eyes.

'You are an assassin?' Katarina asked.

He nodded.

'I have a hunting knife.' She pulled it from a leather sheath on her belt and held it up threateningly.

'I won't hurt you,' the Shadow murmured, a smile playing across his lips. 'I couldn't if I wanted to.'

'You've lost a lot of blood,' Hal's mum said, coming forward and kneeling beside him to look at his injuries.

'I have three bullets in my right leg. Another has passed through my shoulder.' The Shadow reported. 'I need to stop bleeding. Can you help me make a tourniquet?'

Hal's mum looked up, and Hal nodded.

Katarina took off the square scarf that she wore under her

hat to keep her neck warm. 'You can use this.' She passed it to Hal's mum, who began tearing it into strips.

'She has the Kill Code, doesn't she?' Hal asked the man.

The Shadow was deathly pale and shivering. He met Hal's eyes and nodded.

'Given your, er, line of work, you may know more about tourniquets than I do,' Hal's mum said, wrapping one of the strips of cloth around his thigh. The Shadow, through a series of grunts and pointing, instructed her where to tie the bandages to stem the bleeding.

'Hal,' Katarina whispered. 'You must choose. To save this man, we must take him back to the train. He needs to get to a hospital, or he will die.'

'But if we go back, we'll lose the Kill Code.' Hal felt sick.

'He cannot walk. We need to put him on the sledge.'

'You. Boy. Nathaniel's nephew,' the Shadow grunted. 'Come here.'

Hal approached, wary of any sudden moves.

'I owe you my life.' He pushed himself up onto the elbow of his good arm. 'I don't forget a debt.'

'I don't want anything from you,' Hal said, then added, 'Except for you to leave my uncle alone.'

'Your uncle is safe from me, kid.' The Shadow's eyes closed, and he fell back.

'We are going to take you back to the train.'

'No.' The Shadow's eyes snapped open and locked on to Hal's. 'You must leave me.' He raised his hand so that Hal wouldn't interrupt or protest. 'The Chameleon has chartered a boat to take her from Narvik, in Norway, to meet her contact and hand over the Kill Code.' His stare intensified as his brow lowered. 'She must be stopped. You must get it back.'

'If we leave you here,' Hal said quietly, 'you'll die.'

'I may.' The Shadow nodded. 'It's a risk you take in my line of work.' A corner of his mouth lifted in a wry smile. 'I am only one life, boy. The Kill Code will take many.'

'I thought you were hired to get the Kill Code?' Hal frowned.

'No. To stop the Chameleon. Like I told your uncle, I'm one of the good guys.' He laughed but it became a cough and he collapsed back down into the snow. The effort of talking had exhausted him.

Hal's mum turned to Katarina. 'Do you think I could walk with Girjak, like Hal did, holding his reins? Would he follow me?'

Katarina nodded. 'If I show you how to hold his reins, to direct him, and you have this –' she pulled a bundle of the springy lichen from her other pocket – 'he will do whatever you want.'

'You can drive a snowmobile, can't you?' Hal's mum said, taking the lichen.

'Yes . . .' Katarina tipped her head. 'Why?'

Hal spun round. The snowmobile was still out on the ice. 'Mum?'

'Hal, this man needs a doctor and neither you nor I can drive a snowmobile.' She looked at Katarina. 'Do you think you can follow the Chameleon's tracks?'

161

Katarina nodded.

'Will you let me take your sledge back to the train with Girjak?' Hal's mum asked.

'My aunt will be pleased to have him back,' Katarina nodded.

'Then you two must follow the Kill Code on the snowmobile,' Hal's mum said. 'But –' she raised a finger – 'you must promise me that you'll always keep a safe distance between you and that woman. She mustn't know you're following her.'

'Yes. It's time we gave her a taste of her own medicine,' Hal replied, with a grim smile.

'But *only* follow her. Do you hear me? Under no circumstances are you to try and get that code yourselves, do you understand? I don't want you going anywhere near her.' She gestured to the Shadow. 'I don't want you ending up like this.'

'I promise, Mum.'

'Once I've got this man some medical attention, I'll come and find you. Your uncle can explain everything to the police and then they can deal with that *woman*.' She said the word as if it tasted bad.

Katarina sprang into action, removing the rope from the Shadow and unhooking Girjak from the sledge. She and the reindeer set out across the ice towards the snowbike.

'Hal, help me lift him onto the sledge, would you?' Beverly was trying to help the Shadow rise onto his one good leg, but he was heavy.

162

Between them, they got him into the back seat of the sledge. Hal watched his mum arrange the hides around and over the assassin, to cushion any bumps and keep him warm. The Shadow's eyes closed, and Hal exchanged a look with his mum. He could tell that she was worried he wouldn't live long enough to make it to hospital. 'I'll get back to the train as quickly as I can,' she muttered.

Katarina yelled a command to Girjak, and Hal saw that the girl had managed to tie a rope to the snowmobile. The reindeer was pulling it back to shore. Once it was close to the edge of the lake, on thicker ice, Katarina lifted the snow bike back onto its skis. She jumped onto it and turned the key, the engine revved. It was still working.

They worked in swift silence, hooking Girjak back up to the sledge and preparing to go their separate ways.

'Mum?' Hal took her cold hands and looked up into her worried eyes. 'You must tell Uncle Nat what the Shadow said about the Chameleon having chartered a boat. I think the fastest way through the mountains to Narvik is by train. That's the route our train was meant to take. The only way she can catch a train is from the station at Kiruna. Katarina and I will follow her tracks, but I think they will lead us there. I will wait for you and Uncle Nat in Kiruna. I won't go anywhere near the Chameleon. I'll just watch her, from a distance. I promise.'

CHAPTER TWENTY-TWO

SÁMI SISTER

Hal watched his mother tentatively call out to Girjak. The sledge jerked forwards. She regained her balance, gripped the reins and looked over her shoulder in farewell. He gave her an encouraging smile. As he watched her go, he felt a wave of emotion rising in his chest and a prickling at the back of his eyes.

'Come.' Katarina was already astride the snowmobile. Her expression was grim and determined, but there was a glint in her eyes.

Hal hopped on behind her and she fired up the ignition, barely giving him time to settle in his seat before the machine lurched forward, roaring across the snow. The noise of the engine cut through the quiet trees. Katarina gave the occasional shout, pointing out the tracks of the other snowbike. It was heading straight for Kiruna.

Katarina drove swiftly and confidently, avoiding traps and snares. After a while, Hal relaxed enough to take in the beauty of the landscape around him. He risked letting go of one of the side handles to look at his watch. He was surprised to find it was nearly lunchtime. It was impossible to guess the time when the sun didn't rise above the horizon.

As they drove, the sky cleared. Above the treeline the horizon was blushing pink, throwing lilac light on the snow-covered tundra, so that it looked like purple sugar. The world had taken on a magical persona. It looked like a scene from a fairytale. He saw tall, thin trees, Christmas trees, pine trees, fir trees, their branches drooping, heavy with snow. Ferns and bracken were blanketed, making pale lumpen forms that at any second could rise up to become rock trolls. There was no life visible in the snowy landscape – no cattle, no foxes, squirrels, or mammals of any kind. Hal wished he could stop time and get out his watercolours. He wondered if this beautiful light was the sunset on a polar night.

Beginning to feel the biting cold, Hal leaned close to Katarina's back as

they drove onwards. He thought about the woman they were following, the Chameleon. She knew what Hal looked like. She'd been watching him since he'd arrived in Stockholm. He had to be careful that she didn't see him following her or they'd be in trouble. He wondered if she still looked like Heidi. He guessed not. He knew she would be difficult to recognize. He thought about the different disguises she'd

already worn. He needed a way to identify her that wasn't to do with her clothes or her hair. He thought about her eyes. Heidi's were an icy blue, but people could change the colour and shape of their eyes with contact lenses and make-up. What part of a person is impossible to change or hide? *Her jawline is strong*, he thought, *and she has a pointy chin. Her small ears stick out at an angle.* He closed his eyes, going over and over the lines of her face in his imagination, noticing she had three ear-piercing holes in each lobe and a slight break in the line of her nose. He sat up, his eyes opening as an idea popped into his head. The Chameleon knew what Harrison Beck looked like, but what if *he* disguised himself too? She would be on the lookout for a boy with his mum and uncle, not two children. And she'd had no reason to pay attention to Katarina on the train. Would she be able to recognize Hal if he was disguised and with Katarina? He fancied she wouldn't.

Hal spotted railway tracks as they crossed a field of snow. The Chameleon's snowmobile had driven alongside them. He tapped Katarina on the shoulder and indicated that he wanted to stop. He needed to find a disguise before they went into Kiruna.

'You hungry?' Katarina asked after she stopped the snowmobile. She opened her bag and took out a couple of strips of dried brown meat. She took a bite from one and handed the other to Hal.

'Thank you.' Hal gratefully gobbled the delicious salty snack down. 'Mmm, what is this? It's delicious.'

'Dried reindeer,' Katarina replied as she chewed her meat.

Hal coughed in shock. 'What? But I thought you loved reindeer!'

'I do. They're delicious.' Katarina looked at Hal as if he were a curious specimen. 'I am Sámi. We are reindeer herders. We honour the reindeer by using every part of them. My bag is made from their hide, my boots too. We use their antlers and their bones for tools, and –' she took another bite – 'we eat them.' She laughed at Hal's expression. 'Sometimes I think about being a vegetarian,' she said, 'but reindeer taste too good.'

Hal realized as she spoke that he knew almost nothing about the Sámi people. He didn't want to offend Katarina, who was so impressive and brave. 'I'm not a vegetarian,' he said. 'It's just, I've never eaten reindeer before. In England, the only thing we know about reindeer is that they pull Father Christmas's sleigh. I didn't expect them to be tasty!'

Katarina found this funny, and as she laughed, Hal found himself laughing too. He told her his idea about wearing a disguise so that the Chameleon wouldn't recognize him, and a wicked smile flashed across her face.

'I have the perfect disguise for you,' she said with glee. 'We will go to my house.'

'OK.' Hal was alarmed by how pleased with herself Katarina was looking as she revved up the engine. As they whooshed onwards to Kiruna, he had a feeling he wasn't going to like her idea of a perfect disguise.

On the outskirts of the town, sticking out of a snowy

thicket, they spotted the other snowmobile. They parked and went to inspect it.

Hal dropped down, examining the side of the vehicle. 'Look, here. Blood.'

'She must be injured.' Katarina studied the snow around the bike. 'There's no blood in the snow.'

'Maybe she's bandaged it,' Hal guessed. 'We should keep our eyes opened for anyone limping, leaning heavily on their left leg, or any signs of bleeding on their right.'

'How do you know it is her right leg that is injured?'

'This patch of blood on the bike is at thigh height, where her right leg would sit, but no blood has dripped onto the footplate, which would make sense if she was wearing a bandage.'

Katarina raised her eyebrows and looked at Hal with respect.

'We don't know how this woman will disguise herself, but by my reckoning, she's about five foot seven. She has three

piercing holes in each of her ear lobes, a strong jaw with a pointy chin, and small sticky-out ears. Everything else – her hair, the colour of her eyes, her body proportions – she can change.' He looked at Katarina. 'It doesn't matter how brilliant she is at disguise, though, you can't easily hide a leg injury.'

'We will be brilliant at disguise too,' Katarina declared, the sparkle of mischief returning to her eyes.

'We will?'

'Yes. I am going to dress you as my pretty Sámi sister,' Katarina said, and laughed heartily at the look on Hal's face.

'Sister?' Hal shook his head. 'But can't I dress up as your cousin or . . .'

'No. This is a good idea.'

'I don't think so.'

'But she will be looking for a blond English *boy*, not a little Sámi girl with a big sister.'

'Wait, what! Am I the *little* sister?' Hal was getting unhappier by the minute.

'Yes. Because I am taller, and you know nothing about Sámi culture.' Katarina jumped back onto the snowmobile. 'Come on. Let's find you some clothes. I can leave a message for my uncle, letting him know the snowbike is here. He will be pleased. It doesn't look damaged.'

As Hal climbed up behind Katarina, he took note of her clothing: the bright red hat and shawl, the blue dress, thick leggings and reindeer-hide boots. He had a horrible feeling he was going to be the worst, most clumsy-looking Sámi girl Kiruna had ever seen.

CHAPTER TWENTY-THREE

THE SINKING TOWN

'I can't wear that!' Hal exclaimed as Katarina held up a blue dress decorated with a bright-coloured trim, like her own.

'You said you wanted a disguise.' Katarina looked flatly at him. 'No one will suspect you are a little English boy if you wear the gákti.'

'People will stare at me!' Hal protested. 'I can't speak Swedish. What if someone tries to talk to me?'

'Ha! This is Sweden. We don't talk with strangers for no reason. Just avoid eye contact.' She shot him a taunting look. 'But if you are too scared to dress like a girl . . .'

'I'm not scared! Not of dressing like a girl.'

'Good. I will find you some boots. And if anyone does talk to you, just look at the ground and say nothing.'

When Hal stepped out of Katarina's house, he felt self-conscious. He was surprised that in the gákti, hat, shawl, and leggings, he was warmer than in the snow clothes he'd brought to weather the Arctic. There was dried grass inside the boots, which felt weird to walk on, but Katarina said it was warmer than synthetic socks. She had given him a leather bag to keep his sketchbook and pens inside, and he'd slung it across his chest. He was grateful that the strange pink light given off by a shy sun hiding below the horizon was now gone completely, leaving a midnight darkness lit up by dingy electric lights. The polar night was handy if you didn't want to be recognized.

'The tricky thing with using the gákti as a disguise,' Katarina said as they trudged back to the snowmobile, 'is that the design and colours identify you. They tell other Sámi where you're from, which village. It says who you are. Each one is unique.'

'Oh!' Hal looked down at his dress. 'Who am I?'

Katarina giggled. 'Me, when I was younger.'

Hal blushed.

'If anyone asks, I will tell them that we are on our way to the Winter Market in Jokkmokk, and that will explain why we're wearing the gákti.'

'You don't wear gákti all the time?'

'Gákti are traditional outfits for parties, weddings, festivals.' Katarina's expression told Hal he'd asked a dumb question. 'I have everyday clothes too.'

Masquerading as Katarina's little sister, Hal mounted the snowmobile behind her, finding that wearing a skirt limited his legs a little, but he felt a surge of bravery, certain that the Chameleon wouldn't recognize him in these clothes. 'Let's go and find that Kill Code.'

'Where shall we look first?'

'The train station. We know the Chameleon is going to Narvik in Norway. The fastest way is by train. Let's hope we're not too late.'

Katarina gunned the engine. As they rode through Kiruna, Hal saw detached modern houses, painted in yellows and reds, lit up by streetlights. Snow was piled high beside the kerbs, but the roads were mostly clear.

Kiruna station had one platform that was open to the elements. A sculpture of four men carrying an iron girder stood on a brick plinth at its entrance. The star-speckled sky above them was inky black. Above the tracks, electricity wires were suspended between intermittent pylons, providing power for the trains, and looming behind them was the giant snow-covered waste heap of Kiruna's famous mine.

It was plain to see that the station's main function was to transport iron ore from the mine. Two endless lines of black freight wagons stretched along tracks set back from the platform. Hal heard the faint grind and crunch of mining

174

machinery and, in the distance, saw the headlights of diggers slowly climbing the lumpy waste heap.

The station building was yellow and modern, and you had to climb a set of steps to enter. Inside it was warm, and along one wall was a frieze featuring photographs and facts about Kiruna in several languages.

While Katarina went to the ticket desk to ask about trains to Narvik, Hal read the information on the wall. It said that Kiruna was one of Europe's largest iron-ore producers, digging enough out of the ground to generate six Eiffel Towers every day. He guessed that was why the town was sinking.

The wall said that each wagon on the freight trains carried one hundred tonnes of iron ore, valued at around seventeen thousand dollars, and that on average there were sixty-eight wagons per train. Hal did the maths in his head. That made one train of iron ore worth more than a million dollars.

'There are only four passenger trains that go between here and Narvik,' Katarina said. 'Two of them are sleeper trains, but they've been cancelled because of the avalanche. One train went first thing this morning, which means that the Chameleon either travels on the last train, which leaves in ten minutes, or gets the morning train.'

'She won't wait till tomorrow,' Hal said, with certainty, going to the window and looking down over the track.

'What do we do?' Katarina frowned. 'If she gets on that train, she'll be in Narvik tonight, and the Kill Code will be gone.'

Hal considered their options. 'We have to catch that train.'

'Hal! We promised your mother we would only follow.'

'And we are. Following her onto the train. We're disguised, she won't recognize us.' Hal turned to Katarina. 'Look, you don't have to come. You never asked to be mixed up in all of this.'

'Neither did you.'

'But . . . I am now.'

'So am I.' Katarina nodded. 'But, what do we do about your mother?'

'We'll leave a note here. Uncle Nat will bring her straight to the station.' Hal pulled out his sketchbook and wrote a note explaining they'd taken the last train to Narvik.

'But how are you going to give that to them?'

Hal looked at the elderly man behind the ticket counter. 'Do you think he'd pass the note on?'

'Yes, if I ask him, but how will he know who to give the note to?'

'Oh, that's easy.' Hal grinned, tearing the page out of his notebook. He folded it in half and then on the top drew a quick sketch of his mother and Uncle Nat.

'Ha!' Katarina was impressed. She took the note to the ticket attendant and bought two return tickets to Narvik. 'Do you think the Chameleon will be wearing a new disguise?'

'Almost definitely.' Hal pursed his lips as he thought. 'But we have a number of things on our side. Firstly, she doesn't know she's being followed. Secondly, she has the Kill Code now – all she needs to do is get to Narvik, board a ship and her mission's complete – so she won't be on her guard. Thirdly, she is injured . . . and fourthly, she's not looking out for two Sámi girls.'

'Told you it was a good disguise,' Katarina said triumphantly.

With seven minutes to go, the Narvik train emerged from the sidings, its headlights beaming. It had three carriages. Hal and Katarina descended the metal stairs onto the platform where the passengers were waiting. As the red doors of the silver carriages slid open, a female ticket inspector stepped out.

'Be careful,' Katarina whispered, as they boarded the train. 'A wounded animal is more savage.'

'A wounded assassin doubly so,' Hal replied grimly.

CHAPTER TWENTY-FOUR

THE LAST TRAIN TO NARVIK

As Hal stepped into the brightly lit carriage, he was embraced by warm air and a surreal feeling of normality, until he caught sight of his own reflection in the window and remembered he was in disguise. The doors beeped and closed. The journey to Narvik was three hours long. If they went all the way, Hal would end up in Norway, a different country, with no passport and dressed like a Sámi girl. A voice in his head warned him that this was a foolish and dangerous thing to do, but he couldn't let the Kill Code go. He had to get it back.

'Now what?' whispered Katarina as they sat down.

'It's a three-carriage train. She's here somewhere. She must be. We just have to work out which passenger she is.'

'What about that woman with the shawl?' Katarina said, signalling with her eyes. 'Or the girl with the skis?'

'The only person we can be certain *isn't* the Chameleon is the ticket inspector. She was on the train already.' Hal glanced furtively at the other passengers. 'And remember, she's injured.

178

We're looking for someone with a limp.'

'I need to use the bathroom,' Katarina said, getting up. 'I'll see who is in the next carriage.'

As the train rolled along the tracks and the lights of the mine grew distant, Hal pulled out his sketchbook. He looked at the pictures he'd drawn of Heidi. Who was this shapeshifting woman? He was disappointed in himself for not noticing her. He prided himself on being observant, but she'd been there all the time. He'd drawn her countless times and yet he hadn't seen her.

He looked up. Katarina was standing in the aisle, looking agitated.

'Someone is in the bathroom, and they aren't coming out,' she complained. 'I knocked three times . . .' She heard herself and stopped, whispering, 'Oh! do you think it is her?'

'It could be.' Hal slipped his sketchbook back in his bag. 'Let's ask the ticket inspector if the bathroom is out of order.'

Hal and Katarina walked down the train, casually surveying the passengers in each carriage. Hal couldn't see anyone he immediately suspected of being the Chameleon.

The ticket inspector was standing outside the engine cab. Katarina spoke to her in Swedish, asking about the toilet. The inspector frowned and shook her head, marching to the toilet, which was in the middle carriage, and knocking on the door. There was no answer. She called out, but there was no reply. Taking a metal bolt with a square end from her pocket, she slotted it into a hole under the handle and turned it.

Hal was holding his breath as the door opened, but the bathroom was empty except for a carrier bag on the floor. The ticket inspector picked it up and peered in. Looking disgusted, she brought it out, holding it at arm's length, taking it to the bin in the corridor, and threw it away.

Katarina thanked the woman and hurried into the bathroom.

Hal waited until the ticket inspector had left the carriage, then looked around. No one seemed to be paying him any attention. He shuffled over to the bin, pushed it open and drew out the bag. Inside was a wavy blonde wig and a wad of bandages soaked in blood. He dropped it back into the bin, scanning the heads of the passengers in the carriage. He didn't think anyone had seen him. His heart was beating hard against his ribcage. He had suspected the Chameleon would be on this train, but now that he knew she was for sure, he suddenly felt afraid.

'Are you all right?' Katarina asked as she came out of the bathroom.

Hal pulled her into a seat and whispered. 'The Chameleon was in the bathroom before you. That bag was full of bandages and a blonde wig.'

Katarina's eyes widened.

'I think she's sitting in this carriage.' He pulled his sketchbook from the little bag and turned to a blank page. He drew the seats in front of him. 'There are five people in here,' he whispered, marking in five heads. 'There's a young couple next to each other over there, holding hands.

A man in overalls who looks like he's sleeping. A woman in a headscarf reading a book, and a much older woman staring at her.'

Katarina watched his pen dance across the paper. 'Which one do you think is the Chameleon?'

'Wrinkles like that are hard to fake,' said Hal, pointing his pen at the older woman. 'And I think she is cross with the one in the headscarf for reading. I'd guess they're together. Maybe mother and daughter.' He moved his pen to point at the young couple. 'I don't think the Chameleon is one of these two. She hasn't had time to strike up a conversation with anyone, let alone get familiar enough to be holding hands.'

'You think she's the man in the overalls?'

Hal met Katarina's eyes and nodded. 'He's wearing a hat pulled down low, and his collar's turned up, hiding most of his face. And, on a train, everyone leaves sleeping people alone.'

'What do we do?'

'We're going to walk past the man and sit down in the seats directly behind him. And Katarina, you must only speak Swedish to me. If we speak English, she'll realize I'm not really a Sámi girl.'

'OK.' Katarina suddenly looked nervous.

'Let's go,' Hal said, slipping his sketchbook back into his bag.

The pair of them walked up the carriage and Katarina talked in Swedish. Hal had no idea what she was saying, but from her tone, he guessed she was mocking him. As they

181

passed the sleeping man, Hal glanced in his direction, but his head was bowed forward, and his shoulders hunched. It was impossible to make out any of his features. He knew there was only one way to be certain whether this was the Chameleon.

He pointed to a pair of empty seats behind the sleeping man, and Katarina sat down. He followed.

'What now?' she mouthed silently.

Hal put his finger to his lips and, dropping his head

between his legs, he leaned right down, as if he were looking for something he'd dropped on the floor.

Katarina bent down too, watching him curiously. She followed the direction of his eyes. They were both looking at the feet of the sleeping man. He was wearing leather lace-up boots, his navy overall trousers hanging right down to the heel. Hal stared at them fixedly. He noticed there was a lump of bulging cloth just above the left ankle, and then his heart clenched as he saw what he was looking for.

Collecting on the edge of the hem of the right trouser leg was a drop of blood. It dripped onto the floor.

Katarina was looking puzzled, lifting her shoulders in a silent question.

Hal sat back up and speedily drew the boots, the trouser hem, and the drops of blood on the fabric and on the floor, so that she understood. The Chameleon was sitting right in front of them.

CHAPTER TWENTY-FIVE

THE CHAMELEON

Hal grabbed Katarina's arm and stood up, moving away, down the carriage, to the furthest seats. He sat down and turned to the first page of his sketchbook where he'd drawn the train route map from Stockholm to Narvik. He pointed to the station of Abisko. 'It's the next stop,' he whispered.

Katarina nodded.

'If we can get those keys, we could get off there.'

'You said we would only watch and follow.' Katarina shook her head, a look of concern on her face. 'You promised.'

'Abisko is the last station in Sweden. The next stop is Narvik.' Hal pointed to his map. 'If she makes it there with the keys, we won't be able to stop her. This is our last and only chance.'

'But we don't know where the keys are.'

'I think I do,' Hal said, turning to the page with the illustration of the boots he'd just drawn. He worked his pen over the cloth around the left ankle, accentuating the bump and wrinkled cloth.

Katarina blinked. 'You don't know that lump is the keys. It could be . . . bandages.'

'No. Her injury is on her right leg, and what kind of wound would need a bandage that makes a bulge like that? Think about it.' Hal tapped his pen to his temple. 'The Chameleon changes her clothes, her hair, her shoes,' he whispered, 'but not her socks.' He paused to let Katarina absorb this. 'The Shadow had knives strapped to his ankles, but this bulge doesn't look like a weapon. It looks like a bunch of keys shoved into a sock.'

Katarina was sceptical. She bent down, looking under the seats again, to see for herself. When she eventually sat back up, she nodded. 'OK.'

Hal looked at his watch. They would be approaching Abisko soon. He carefully thought through what he intended to do. He leaned close to Katarina and whispered the plan into her ear. When he drew back, he could see she was frightened, but she nodded her agreement. What he was intending was desperate and risky, but it might work, and besides, he was out of ideas.

Getting to her feet, Katarina went to the other end of the carriage and stood by the luggage rack. She stared out of the window, watching the snowy embankment fly by.

Hal's chest was tight as he slipped back into the seat behind the Chameleon. He put his sketchbook down and sat, alert, and waited for the signal from Katarina.

As the train approached Abisko, Katarina grabbed a hard-cased wheelie suitcase from the luggage rack and came back down the aisle towards the Chameleon's seat. It was the sign

186

for Hal to drop to the floor.

Kneeling in the footwell, Hal reached his hands forward, under the seat in front, holding them close to the Chameleon's ankle where he prayed the keys were hidden.

He heard Katarina make a noise, as if stumbling. There was a clatter and she cried out in Swedish. Hal saw the Chameleon's injured leg jerk, and a violently suppressed roar of pain came from the assassin. As fast as lightning, he lifted the left trouser leg, pulled at the thick sock and lifted the keys from their hiding place. He didn't have a second to feel victorious; his heart was beating as fast as a hummingbird's. He crawled backwards, and pushed himself to his feet.

Katarina was apologizing profusely to the Chameleon in Swedish. The young man from the romantic couple stood up, pointing at the suitcase she had dropped onto the assassin's bad leg. It was obviously his. Katarina held up her hands and shook her head, pretending to be embarrassed, and began to back away down the aisle. Hal followed.

We did it! Hal thought, gripping the keys as he made his way along the aisle. The train halted and the doors beeped open. *We're going to escape!*

'Hej!' A woman said. He felt a hand grip his shoulder, stopping him.

Hal's heart hammered as he turned, terrified he'd find himself looking into the eyes of the Chameleon, but it was the ticket inspector, holding out his sketchbook. He'd left it on the seat.

'Err . . . sorry, thank you,' Hal muttered, grabbing it and

stuffing it in his bag, then lurching after Katarina out the door, stepping onto the snowy platform of Abisko station and gulping down deep breaths of crisp cold air. Katarina wordlessly took his hand and they walked away from the train together, resisting the urge to run.

The blood in Hal's head was pounding so loudly he could hear nothing else. He glanced at Katarina. Her eyes were wide, her jaw was tight, she was gritting her teeth. Her hand was almost crushing his, but in his left fist he clutched Morti's keys. They'd done it. They'd got the Kill Code back.

As they made their way down the platform towards the exit, the carriage doors beeped and slid closed behind them. Hal risked a glance over his shoulder. No one else had got off the train. Relief turned his knees to jelly. They paused, turning as the train to Narvik slowly started moving, gliding away.

'We did it!' Katarina whispered in astonishment, leaning against him with relief.

Hal's heart soared, and to his surprise there were tears in his eyes. He opened his lips to speak, then froze as his joy and relief became ashes in his mouth.

As the last carriage rolled away, he saw a dark figure standing on the other side of the tracks. Hal immediately recognised the miner's overalls and dark woollen hat. The Chameleon stood calmly, looking at them with a murderous expression on her face.

'Katarina,' Hal gasped. 'Run!'

Katarina didn't move. Her eyes were fixed on the assassin.

'Children.' The Chameleon tutted. 'There is nowhere for

you to run to.'

Hal looked about desperately, hoping to see someone who could help, but the station appeared to be unstaffed and the platform was deserted: the lone strip of snow-covered concrete was flanked on both sides by railway tracks. Beyond the lit edges of the station was only darkness. This was an isolated place. They were trapped.

'Go,' Hal hissed, giving Katarina a gentle push. 'Run! Get

away.'

But Katarina didn't move.

The Chameleon slowly walked forward, stepping over the rails. She was leaning heavily on her left leg, limping. 'I think you'd better give me back those keys, don't you?'

Hal and Katarina retreated along the platform. Hal thought about denying having the keys, but her eyes were fixed on his left fist.

'Let me make this crystal clear,' she said, stepping up onto the platform and turning to face them. 'If you try anything clever, I will kill you.'

CHAPTER TWENTY-SIX

AURORA BOREALIS

Towering mountains stood around the station like silent witnesses in the dark. Hal could see a huddle of red-painted houses set back from the other side of the tracks, too far to reach or hear a cry. He searched the hostile landscape for any sign of help but saw nothing and no one. They were on their own.

'I underestimated you, Harrison Beck.' The assassin spoke with a clipped European accent. 'Yours is a strange disguise, but clever. I didn't recognize you until you gave yourself away.' She imitated Hal's stumbling words to the ticket inspector, '*Err . . . sorry, thank you!*' and flashed him a sardonic smile. 'What Sami girl speaks English with a British accent?'

Hal's heart sank as he realized his mistake, but the hopelessness of this situation seemed to be having a calming effect on his nerves and focusing his mind. The worst had already happened, they'd been caught, but they were alive, and he still held the Kill Code. His brain fired options and possibilities at him.

The Chameleon reached out a hand.

'Keys. Now.'

'The Kill Code will become a deadly weapon.' Hal's fingers gripped the keys tightly. 'Do you want that?'

'Kid, you're confusing me with someone who has a conscience.' She snorted. 'And besides –' one side of her mouth lifted in a sneer – 'I like weapons.'

'Innocent people will die,' Hal protested.

'It happens.' She hobbled a step closer. 'And if you don't give me those keys, it's going to happen right now.'

Hal's throat was dry, his eyes darting around in the dark, frantically searching for an escape. He needed more time.

'You're trapped,' the Chameleon said, seeming to read his mind. 'Just give me the keys and I'll let you go.'

'You won't,' Katarina snarled.

The Chameleon laughed and shrugged. 'You're right. No, I won't.' Tiring of the exchange, she reached behind her and pulled out a pistol with a silencer attached and pointed it at Hal. 'Keys.'

Hal stared at the gun. Time seemed to stop and all his senses intensified.

Suddenly the infinite star-speckled darkness above them was flooded with a wave of green light, rising and fading like the breaking tide.

'Would you look at that.' The Chameleon lifted her chin. 'The Aurora Borealis is putting on a show for you.'

But Hal wasn't looking at the sky. The green glow of the Northern Lights had revealed a darkness in the distance.

He saw the outline of something coming down the tracks towards them: a small but growing black square. A train was approaching. Hal realized immediately that he must stall for time.

'This . . . this isn't how my uncle planned for me to see the Northern Lights,' he stammered. 'We were supposed to come to Abisko together. It was my Christmas present.'

'Oh, boo-hoo.' The Chameleon sighed. 'You shouldn't have come running after me then, should you?' She jerked the gun. 'Keys.'

Hal held up his left fist and took a step towards her. He worked to keep her looking at him. He didn't want her to turn around. 'You don't need her.' He nodded at Katarina. 'Why don't you let her go? She's got nothing to do with any of this.'

'I'm afraid I can't do that. I can't have people walking about who can identify me, which is why I'll be taking your sketchbook too.'

'Why were you following us in Stockholm?' Hal asked, edging closer.

'I knew Dr Sorenson had the code on a ring. I was told she kept it on a necklace. When I didn't find it in her possessions, I followed her, hoping she'd lead me to it. But then she disappeared from the hotel in the night.'

'It was you who stole my uncle's phone and room key, wasn't it?'

'Yes. I searched your room. I thought Dr Sorenson might have given the ring to him for safekeeping. You almost caught me.' She raised an eyebrow. 'I had to make a noise to get you to follow your uncle back down to reception, so that I could get out.'

Hal shivered at the thought that the Chameleon had been standing on the other side of his hotel room door, listening.

'That's how I discovered your uncle had booked Dr Sorenson a ticket on the night train as far as Kiruna. She'd left a message on his phone, asking him to do it. When I discovered Dr Sorenson had checked out of the hotel in the night, I decided to follow your uncle, and learn what I could.'

'Why did you try to take his wallet?'

'If I have a person's credit cards, I can find out what they've been buying. I thought the night train might be a ruse, a bluff to send me on a wild goose chase. I wanted to be sure he'd bought Dr Sorenson a ticket.' A look of begrudging respect crossed her face. 'Your uncle is famous for pulling that kind of trick.'

'You know him?'

She shook her head. 'I do my research.'

'When did you work out that the Kill Code was on the key ring?' Hal asked, keeping his eyes fixed on hers and trying to ignore the growing shadow behind her.

'Oh, you told me.' The Chameleon smiled. 'Imagine my surprise when your mother proudly shows me your sketchbook, and in all the pictures, there I am! I studied each of your drawings, and lo and behold, dangling from the key fob, was an engraved ring. I might never have worked it out. Thanks for that. It was a big help.'

Hal felt sick. The Chameleon had worked out where the Kill Code was from his picture before he had.

'Ha!' She saw his dismay. 'Sorry, kid.'

'How did you get into Morti's lab window without her camera seeing you?' Hal asked, clutching at subjects to keep the Chameleon talking. He could hear the rails vibrating as the black locomotive approached.

'I didn't climb in through the window. I came in through the air-conditioning vent, in the ceiling, behind the camera. I pressed pause, unlocked and opened the window, and let it carry on recording.' She snorted. 'A simple but effective bit of misdirection.'

'You have missed the last train to Narvik,' Katarina said, and Hal knew she must have seen the oncoming train. 'You will not be able to reach your boat today.'

'You know about that, do you?' The Chameleon looked surprised. 'Thank you for telling me. I'll be sure to take a different route. I don't want to run into any more . . . setbacks.'

'Won't your employer be waiting for the ring?' Katarina asked.

'I'm sure an extra day or two won't trouble him.'

'Björn!' Hal exclaimed. 'You were hired by Björn, Morti's husband!'

'Quite the detective, aren't we?' she said sourly.

'You're going to kill us anyway,' Hal said, almost shouting to try and cover the sound of the approaching locomotive.

'What do you care what we know?'

'True. But you should have worked that out ages ago, detective boy. If it wasn't Björn who hired me, Dr Mortimer Sorenson would have been dead months ago. Sentimental fool wouldn't let me kill her.' She shook her head as if this made no sense and raised her gun. 'Now, give me those keys.'

The black engine was fast approaching the platform, and a spark of hope ignited in Hal's chest as he realized that it didn't have its headlights on. He held up the keys as if he were about to throw them, but then paused and pointed. 'Look! There's a train coming. You should put your gun away or someone will see you pointing it at two Sámi girls.'

The Chameleon tipped her head as if she couldn't believe what Hal was saying. 'Do you really think I'm that stupid? That I'll fall for the *It's behind you* trick? What are you going to do when I turn around? Throw a snowball at me and run?' She took a step towards him, and Hal saw that she was trying to hide how much pain her injured leg was causing her.

Risking a glance at the oncoming locomotive, Hal thought he could make out one figure in the cab, and a familiar silhouette leaning out of the open door.

'There *is* a train coming,' Katarina said, pointing.

'I know there's a train coming,' the Chameleon snapped. 'I can hear it and I don't care! Give me the keys *now*.' She moved the gun so that it pointed at Katarina. 'Or I'll shoot your friend.'

Katarina gasped.

'NO! Please don't.' Hal walked forward holding out the keys. 'Here you are. Take them.'

CHAPTER TWENTY-SEVEN

PLATFORM ALTERCATION

As Hal approached the Chameleon, she started to turn her head, to look back at the oncoming locomotive. He knew if the assassin saw Uncle Nat hanging out of the open door of the engine cab, she would shoot at him. Yelling with all his might, he ran at her, using his elbow to strike her injured thigh as hard as he could. He hoped she would crumple to the ground, but her weight was on her left leg. Instead, she roared with pain, her head snapping back, glaring at him with rage-filled eyes.

Her free hand swung, grabbing Hal around the neck, getting him in a headlock. He saw the barrel of the gun moving towards him, but before she could point it, Hal heard a furious cry.

The world pitched and turned as both he and the Chameleon were knocked to the ground by the flying figure of Uncle Nat, who had leaped from the moving locomotive. As Hal hit the snow, Morti's keys flew out of his hand.

'Hal, get on the train!' Uncle Nat shouted.

'The keys!' Hal exclaimed.

The Chameleon scrambled backwards like a crab, her gun in one hand, waving wildly in Uncle Nat's direction, her other hand reaching blindly behind her for the keys. Hal sat up in time to see Katarina sprint forwards, grab the keys, pivot, and race towards the engine which was screeching and shuddering to a stop.

The Chameleon cursed in a language Hal didn't recognize. She turned and aimed her gun at Katarina's back, but Hal was already hurling his leg upwards with all his might. He kicked the weapon out of her hand. It fell to the ground, in the snow.

'Hal, get out of here!' Uncle Nat roared, lunging towards the gun as the Chameleon sprang up onto her left leg. They froze, two metres apart, glaring intensely at each other, poised to move if the other so much as flinched. The gun lay somewhere between them, invisible in the snow.

Hal tore himself away and sprinted to the engine cab, which had ground to a halt at the other end of the platform. Ahead of him, he saw Katarina climb inside and a moment later he was scrambling up the ladder, hurling himself through the door and onto the floor.

'I got the keys.' Katarina held them up, her eyes wide. She looked wild with fear.

'Well done,' Hal panted. His heart was beating like a theatre of stamping feet. 'Erik!' he exclaimed in surprise as he spotted Alfred's dad in the driving seat of the engine. Erik grunted, but he was wrestling with the controls. He put the train into reverse and very slowly backed along the platform. Hal went to the window. He heard Erik suck in a breath as they both saw the Chameleon throw a punch at Uncle Nat. But he dodged her fist, throwing a punch of his own and as she stumbled backwards, recovering her balance, her hat fell to the ground revealing a shaved head and a tattoo of a snake coiled around her skull.

'She's trying to create an opening so she can grab her gun,' Hal said, as the engine reversed past them.

'What's he going to do?' Katarina asked as they moved to look through the windscreen at the two tense figures on the platform.

'Why aren't you stopping?' Hal snapped at Erik as the engine continued to draw back, away from the fighting pair.

'Nathaniel told me, that once you were on the train, I was to get moving,' Erik said, his mouth a grim line.

Hal didn't argue, but he lurched forward, lifted and pushed the lever on the dashboard, putting on the brakes, and twisting a switch to put the engine in neutral. 'The Kill Code is here. We're here,' Hal said forcefully, glaring into Erik's eyes. 'All Uncle Nat has to do is get aboard. I'm not leaving him. It would be a death sentence.'

Erik nodded and Hal could see that he was afraid.

Hal turned back to Uncle Nat and the Chameleon. They were staring at each other. Could Uncle Nat defeat her? The Chameleon had beaten the Shadow and left him for dead, but now she was injured. Hal felt nauseous with worry. He knew, even hurt, that the assassin was deadly.

200

Suddenly his uncle moved, hopping forwards on his left leg with his fists high, as if he were going to punch the Chameleon. She danced back a step, lifting her fists to a defensive position in front of her face and Hal saw a shining silver knuckleduster on her right hand. But Uncle Nat didn't throw a punch. Instead he stepped his right leg forward, stomping his foot down two or three times before it landed on the gun. Realizing what he'd done, the Chameleon's face twisted in anger, and she struck him with a powerful uppercut that connected with Uncle Nat's jaw. Hal gasped as he saw his uncle fold, thinking she had knocked him down, but then he saw his uncle's hand drop to his right foot. When he rose back up, he was clutching the barrel of the gun. In one swift continuous movement, he lifted the gun high over his shoulder and hurled it metres away into a deep bank of snow.

The Chameleon let out a guttural growl of anger, darting forward and punching Uncle Nat in the ribs. Hal watched his uncle double over as she raised her hand to strike him again, the platform light reflecting off the silver knuckleduster. But before she could hit him, Uncle Nat struck out at her injured thigh. The Chameleon saw the move coming and spun around on her good leg, executing a roundhouse kick with her injured leg that sent Uncle Nat flying backwards.

The Chameleon cried out in pain but was already turning and staggering towards the snowdrift to get her gun.

Uncle Nat landed heavily but, to Hal's surprise, he sprang up and kicked hard at the back of the Chameleon's knee. Her good leg collapsed, and she fell forward, hitting the ground face first, letting out a howl of rage.

Uncle Nat pivoted, sprinting towards the locomotive cab shouting, 'GO! GO! GO!'

Hal twisted the knob on the driver's console, to put the engine into gear, lifted the lever and pulled it towards him. He looked at Erik, saying, 'All yours,' before rushing to the door, where Katarina was standing looking out.

Uncle Nat ran along the platform towards them, reaching the moving door and grabbing on to the railing, getting a foot on the ladder and hauling himself up into the cab. Hal and Katarina grabbed at his coat and pulled him in.

'She's coming!' Erik called out.

The Chameleon was back on her feet and clutching her gun. She hobbled forward at a furious pace, her face a picture of focused rage. She jumped down onto the tracks, running towards them.

'How is she doing that?' Katarina wondered in horror.

'Speed up, Erik, speed up!' Uncle Nat said.

The Chameleon lifted her gun and took aim.

'Down! Everybody! Get down on the floor!' Uncle Nat said, ducking below the control desk.

Hal dropped to the floor as he heard glass breaking and bullets hitting the wall above him. He saw the end of Abisko's platform move past the open door. The engine was travelling quite fast now.

Uncle Nat risked lifting his head, to peer out of the windscreen. When he didn't duck back down, Hal felt emboldened to look.

The Chameleon had stopped running. She was standing between the tracks, glaring at the disappearing train with a burning fury.

'We got away,' Hal whispered in disbelief. 'We did it!'

'And we've got the Kill Code,' Katarina added.

'Are you OK?' Hal asked his uncle.

'I am now,' said Uncle Nat, pulling a handkerchief from his pocket and pressing it to his face where the Chameleon's knuckleduster had cut his skin. He winced. 'I'm fine now that I know you two are all right. When both of you and Bev went chasing after two assassins, I almost had kittens!'

Hal didn't know why, but this made him laugh, and once he'd started laughing, he couldn't stop, for fear he would start crying.

Uncle Nat put an arm around him and gave him a gentle hug. 'It's all over now,' he said softly.

'It's not.' Hal raised his head. 'It won't be over until we've destroyed the Kill Code.'

'Erik has an idea about how we can do that, don't you, Erik?'

'At the mine, there is a blast furnace in the processing plant,' Erik said. 'You might have seen it beyond Kiruna station. It is a giant brick shed at the end of the tracks. That is where the pellets of iron are made and cooled, before they're poured into the wagons that are hitched to the engines that pull it to Narvik.'

Hal thought of the long lines of freight wagons he'd seen at Kiruna and nodded. 'The ring needs to be utterly destroyed.'

'The blast furnace will melt almost anything.' Erik smiled.

Katarina handed Hal the keys. He unclipped the popper holding the ring on the fob and slipped it off, giving the keys to his uncle. Staring at the gold band, he glimpsed the numbers inside it, but he didn't want to know what they were. He closed his fist, wondering that something so small could cause so much trouble.

'At least we've got rid of that . . . creature,' Erik said, bringing the locomotive down to a safe driving speed and switching the headlights on.

'We don't know that,' Uncle Nat said, and then seeing the alarmed look on Hal and Katarina's face, he added, 'But there's no way she can catch us now. She's injured and has no mode of transport. Plus, it's freezing out there and there are no more passenger trains until morning. We'll be back in Kiruna in an hour, and we'll go straight to the mine.'

CHAPTER TWENTY-EIGHT

INTO THE FIRE

Hal and Katarina were quiet on the journey back to Kiruna. They were sitting together on a double seat at the back of the cabin.

'I'm sorry, I've got your gákti dirty.' Hal rubbed at a mark on the skirt. 'I'll wash it when we get to the cabin.'

'You will not,' Katarina said. 'I let you wear it, but I don't trust you to wash it. I will clean it myself.'

Hal wasn't sure whether to be offended or flattered, and Uncle Nat chuckled.

'Uncle Nat, where did you and Erik get this locomotive?' Hal asked, looking at the bullet holes in the windscreen.

'Um . . .' Uncle Nat glanced sideways at Erik. 'We sort of borrowed it, from the mine. It's a class thirty-four, used for pulling the freight wagons.'

'You stole a locomotive!' Hal couldn't help but grin.

'Look, you went after a trained killer, despite promising your mother you wouldn't. I didn't have much of a choice.'

'Where is Mum? Is she cross?'

'She's waiting for us at the station in Kiruna. And she's not cross, she's terrified.'

'What happened to the Shadow?' Hal asked. 'Did he die?'

'He was alive when he was loaded into one of the ambulances that came to the train crash.'

'Was Girjak OK?' Katarina asked.

'Girjak?'

'Katarina's reindeer,' Hal explained.

'Your aunt was very pleased to get him and the sledge back. Your uncle was proud that you went after the snowmobiles.'

Katarina smiled at this.

'Why are we driving backwards?' Hal asked.

'It is my brother who drives trains,' Erik confessed. 'We drove forwards to get to Abisko, and I don't know how we can turn, so we will have to go backwards to Kiruna.'

'We worked most of the controls out on the way to find you,' Uncle Nat admitted. 'We were trying to catch up with the passenger train. I never dreamed I'd see you on the Abisko platform. I thought you'd stay on the train to Narvik.'

'We managed to get the keys. We were trying to escape, but she came after us.'

Hal slipped into a daze as they journeyed back to Kiruna. It seemed to take no time at all, and when he got up to disembark, every muscle in his body ached. He swayed on his feet, overcome with tiredness. His uncle noticed and helped him climb down the ladder onto the snow-covered ballast by the side of the track.

'This isn't the station.' Hal looked round, confused. They

207

were in a row of sidings, lit by floodlights. Long lines of empty freight wagons rested on a parallel track.

'We've gone past the station,' Uncle Nat explained. 'These are the marshalling yards that belong to the mine.' He pointed at a towering, windowless building beyond the tracks.

'Hal!'

His heart leaped at the sound of his mother's voice. She ran towards them across the tracks. Her arms were outstretched. She gathered him in for a hug. 'You're OK!' She put an arm around Katarina too, who stiffened at the gush of emotion. 'Are you OK?'

They both nodded.

'I was so worried.' Hal's mum bit her bottom lip. 'Did you do it? Did you get the keys?'

Hal opened his fist and showed her Morti's wedding ring.

'Oh, well done,' she looked from Hal to Katarina and back to Hal. 'You brave, heroic, idiots. Don't you ever do anything like that again.'

Hal could tell she was proud and trying not to cry.

'Let's get this over and done with, shall we?' Uncle Nat said, turning towards the huge warehouse with a determined expression. 'Lead on, Erik.'

The five of them – Hal, Katarina, Uncle Nat, Mum and Erik – marched across the icy ballast towards the giant silhouette of the iron-ore processing plant. The rails led right up to a line of buffers by the wall of the building, where a door, seeming tiny in the huge structure, was lit by a glowing overhead lamp.

Hal heard a high vibration and looked down at the rails beside his feet. They were singing to him. It was a warning that something was coming. He looked over his shoulder into the darkness, but the floodlights made it hard to see anything beyond the marshalling yard. His stomach felt tight, and his heart fluttered. *I'm just tired*, he told himself, *my mind is playing tricks on me.*

'I think we should hurry,' he said, picking up his pace and walking to the door ahead of the others. He tried the handle. It was locked.

'You need a keycard to open it,' said Erik, patting his pockets. 'Hold on.'

Uncle Nat turned to look back. He'd heard the noise from the rails too. 'What on earth is that?' He muttered to himself, and they all looked.

Barrelling through Kiruna station, coming round the bend at a furious speed, was a locomotive pulling a string of freight wagons.

'That's the freight train from Narvik . . .' Erik said. He frowned. 'But it shouldn't be going that fast.'

'It's her!' Hal gasped. 'It's the Chameleon!' Instinctively, he knew he was right. 'She's trying to stop us from destroying the ring!'

'Erik, open that door,' Hal's mum instructed.

Erik fumbled with his keycard, holding it against a reader, which flashed green.

'She's coming straight towards us!' Katarina exclaimed.

Hal glanced back and saw the freight train piling down the

209

siding, hurtling along the tracks. It wasn't slowing down.

Erik yanked the door open. 'Inside!' He barked.

Hal's mum grabbed him and Katarina, bundling them through the door into the warehouse. Uncle Nat hurried in after them, shutting the door.

They were on the open floor of the processing plant, covered with a maze of machinery that rumbled and hissed. All the lights were on, and Hal saw workers in overalls on metal gangways above them.

'Up here,' said Erik, running to some iron steps. 'The furnace is on the other side of . . .'

Hal heard a deafening *clang!* followed by a caterwauling of friction screams and crashing metal as the warehouse wall behind them exploded into a shower of bricks. A shockwave swept through the floor like an earthquake and Hal's knees buckled, as a locomotive came hurtling through the building towards them, its wheels sending up showers of sparks.

Hal threw himself forward, after Erik and his mum, then heard her call his uncle's name. He saw Uncle Nat grab Katarina, dragging her back out of the engine's path. The two of them rolled to safety as a string of empty freight wagons cannoned across the floor behind the loco, cutting them off from view.

The train tore down pillars and smashed into machinery as it came to a stop with excruciating slowness. Lights flickered, and a klaxon wailed.

Hal stared at the wreckage in horror, his ears ringing.

'You have to take me to the furnace,' he shouted above the din, stumbling towards Erik.

'It's her!' Hal's mum cried.

Following his mum's eyes, Hal saw the Chameleon climbing from the wreckage of the locomotive. She dropped from the cab onto the floor, blood running down her face, gun in her hand. His heart lurched in fear.

'Now!' He yelled at Erik.

Erik sprinted away from the wreckage, leading Hal and his mum onto a metal gangway that clanked beneath their feet. They ducked between hissing pipes and dangling chains, until they emerged in a cavernous room dominated by a giant machine. Hal felt himself collide with a wall of heat.

'Pelletizing plant!' Erik shouted above the roar of machinery. 'Don't touch anything!'

The temperature was almost unbearable. Erik passed Hal's mum a helmet, taken from a hook on the wall. He put one on Hal's head and flipped the visor down to protect his face. He pointed, and Hal saw the mouth of the furnace, liquid metal as bright as the sun in its gullet. Hal shielded his eyes, gripping the ring so hard it cut into his skin. He'd never wanted to destroy anything more in his life.

Thousands of grey, marble-sized, iron pellets were being carried along a huge conveyor belt into the blazing hot mouth of the oven, where they flushed red. That was where he had to throw the ring. He forged forwards, holding an arm up to shield himself from the bright light and the intense heat.

He heard his mum cry out behind him and spun around.

A bolt of fear struck him as he saw the Chameleon in the doorway. Erik lay face down on the ground.

His mum hurled herself at the assassin, grappling for her gun.

Hal froze.

'DO IT!' shouted his mother as she struggled with the Chameleon.

Hal couldn't move.

'DO IT RIGHT NOW!' His mother's voice had taken on the tone that she used when he was in serious trouble, and suddenly he was running towards the furnace. He made the mistake of glancing back as the Chameleon struck his mother and he saw her crumple, slumping to the ground.

'NO!' Hal screamed.

The Chameleon turned to look at Hal. She gave him a catlike smile, staggering towards him. One dragging step, then another. Her gun pointing at his head.

Hal knew that he was going to die. This was it. Mum's premonition had been right. He was never going home again.

Then, behind the advancing assassin, silently rising up with a face like thunder, was his mum. She grabbed at a long iron chain that hung from a giant machine and whirled it around her head.

'Throw me the ring, and I won't kill you,' the Chameleon shouted, just as his mum let go of the chain. It whipped into the side of the assassin's head, knocking her right off her feet.

Hal watched in shock as the Chameleon's body flew, landing heavily on the floor.

'HAL, THROW THAT DAMN RING INTO THE
FURNACE RIGHT NOW!' his mother howled.

And Hal turned, hurling the gold circle engraved with the
Kill Code into the mouth of the furnace. He watched it travel
into the heat amongst the iron-ore balls. It blazed, became a
shining caramel liquid, and was then gone, forever.

CHAPTER TWENTY-NINE

JOURNEY'S END

Hal tore off the visor and ran to his mum, falling into her arms. His face was wet with tears.

'It's all right. It's all right,' his mother said softly, stroking his hair. 'You're OK. I'm here.' The thunderous noise of the machines around him was so loud that Hal let himself sob.

'Come on now,' Hal's mum encouraged him. 'We need to find Nathaniel and Katarina. They might need our help.'

Hal wiped his eyes and blinked, nodding.

Erik was sitting up, rubbing the back of his head. Hal's mum helped him to his feet, and the three of them made their way back to the train crash. The heap of metal creaked and ticked and Hal was astonished by the great gouges it had made in the concrete floor.

Hal spotted Uncle Nat's head peering over the barrier of wreckage and saw the relief on his face when he spied the three of them coming towards him.

'What happened?' Uncle Nat called out, his eyes flashing with concern. 'Where's the Chameleon?'

'Mum took care of her,' Hal replied with a grin. 'Where's Katarina?'

'Sitting down. She's turned her ankle.'

Katarina's face popped up. 'Did you melt the ring?'

Hal nodded. 'The Kill Code is gone.'

They heard sirens, and the shouting voices of police and paramedics filled the place as people came running in through the hole in the wall. They fanned out, looking for the wounded and to inspect the damage.

'We need to tell them about the Chameleon,' Hal said. 'They have to arrest her, before she wakes up and gets away.'

'I'll take them,' said Erik. He called out to them in Swedish, beckoning them to the gangway.

Hal and his mum clambered over the wreckage to get to Uncle Nat and Katarina.

'The police are here,' Hal told Katarina.

'I should tell them what has happened,' she said. 'They will have many questions.'

'Where is the Chameleon?' Uncle Nat asked him.

'Out cold, in the furnace room,' Hal said. 'Mum knocked her out. She fought with her and took her down with a chain lasso, like Wonder Woman!'

His mum blushed. 'She was pointing a gun at Hal's head!'

'Wait till I tell Dad what you did,' Hal said. 'He'll never grumble when you tell him to put out the bins ever again.'

'Erm . . .' His mum frowned. 'Actually, I'd rather your father didn't know some of the things that happened today. It would only worry him.' She looked from Hal to Nat. 'And the three of us are all right, right now, aren't we?'

'Yes. We are,' Uncle Nat replied, smiling at Hal.

A pair of medics came over and looked at Katarina's ankle.

'It's just a sprain. They say we should go outside,' she told Hal. 'The ambulances are there, and they will be able to bandage my ankle.'

Hal's mum and Uncle Nat each put a shoulder under Katarina's arms and half carried her outside to the ambulance.

'Mum, look!' Hal pointed to the sky. 'The Northern Lights.'

'The Aurora Borealis,' Uncle Nat said. 'Created by particles from storms on the surface of the sun, travelling towards Earth and colliding with its magnetic field.'

'The sun is sending a message to us in our hour of darkness,' Katarina said, as a medic strapped up her ankle. 'Light is here, even if we can't see it, and it will rise again. Soon.'

Hal thought the unearthly rippling green and purple light looked like magic made visible.

After the police had taken their details, it was agreed that they could go. Uncle Nat shepherded them all towards a taxi, declaring it was time to go to the cabin. 'Where do you live, Katarina? We'll take you home first.'

'No. I will drive my snowmobile home,' Katarina declared. 'It is not far.'

'Are you sure?' Hal said. 'What about your ankle?'

'I am certain. I don't need my ankle to drive the snowmobile. I will enjoy telling my cousin all about today.' She lifted her chin.

'He'll never make you ride in the sledge again.' Hal laughed.

'Do you think you'll stay till tomorrow?' Katarina asked. 'It's the Festival of St Lucia. There is a procession at the Ice Hotel with singing and music. Will you come? I'm one of the handmaidens.'

'I will,' Hal promised. 'I think the Dynamic Dozen are playing.'

They watched Katarina climb aboard her snowmobile and fire up the motor, waving as she drove away.

'Look,' said Hal's mum, pointing behind them. They turned to see the Chameleon, in handcuffs, being wrestled into the back of a police car by three officers. They slammed the door on her, and drove her away.

'What will happen to her?' Hal asked.

'She is wanted in several countries for a series of crimes,' Uncle Nat said. 'I think she'll find herself in a prison cell for the rest of her life.'

'Good,' Hal's mum said.

Uncle Nat put an arm around his sister, and an arm around Hal. Nobody spoke for a moment as they stood looking up at the Northern Lights.

'I think you destroyed your premonition, like you destroyed the Chameleon,' Hal said to his mum. 'By becoming Wonder Woman.'

'We control our own fate,' his mum said, then smiled. 'And you should never underestimate an angry mum.'

CHAPTER THIRTY

THE FESTIVAL
OF LIGHTS

H al sat up, confused. It was dark. He could hear singing. When he opened his bedroom door, he found his mum humming to herself as she made coffee in the kitchen of Morti's cabin.

'Morning,' she said cheerfully.

'I don't think I'll ever get used to it being dark in daytime,' Hal said, through a yawn. 'Is it early?'

'It's eleven.' His mum smiled, looking at him affectionately. 'You've slept for hours. Your uncle's still asleep.'

'You're in a good mood.'

'I had a sauna this morning. And, when you aren't scared out of your wits, this place –' she waved at the window, through which Hal could see Kiruna – 'is simply beautiful.'

Hal went to the cabin door and opened it. *I'm here*, he thought, with a smile, *in the Arctic, with Mum and Uncle Nat. We made it!*

'Morning.' Uncle Nat stumbled out of his bedroom. 'Is that coffee?' he asked, bleary-eyed. 'I need coffee.'

'I'll wake you up.' Hal gathered a handful of snow from the doorstep, packed it into a tight ball, spun round and threw it at Uncle Nat, who ducked.

It smashed against the wall.

Uncle Nat grinned. 'You're going to have to get out of bed earlier than that if you want to catch—'

The second snowball hit him squarely on the chin.

Hal collapsed into a fit of giggles, and his mum laughed at the shock on Uncle Nat's face.

'Oh! That's unpleasant.' He grimaced. 'There's icy water dripping down my neck.'

Hal held his stomach as he bent double, laughing hard.

'You just wait, young Harrison,' Uncle Nat said, pretending to be stern. 'I'm a champion snowballer.'

'The Festival of Lights is taking place at the Ice Hotel this afternoon,' Hal's mum said.

'We have to go,' Hal said. 'I promised Katarina.'

'I believe,' Uncle Nat reached out to receive a cup of coffee as Hal came back inside, 'the Dynamic Dozen are playing. They're staying at the hotel.'

'Yes, Birgitta told me they were.' Hal felt a fizz of excitement, and noticed it was the nice kind, which came from anticipating something fun, and not the terrifying kind that heralded adventure. 'It's going to be great.'

'Nat, have you decided what you want to do about travelling home?' his mum asked. 'Hal is meant to go to school tomorrow, but I've sent a message saying that our train was derailed due to an avalanche, and he won't be able to attend.'

'Best excuse ever,' Hal said with a grin.

'We were meant to be flying this evening, but we haven't done half of the things I'd hoped we might.' Uncle Nat looked apologetically at Hal. 'We never did get to go to the Aurora Sky Station in Abisko.'

'No but I went to the train station,' Hal replied, going over to the table and sitting down in front of his sketchbook and watercolours. 'And we saw the Northern Lights.' Hal flipped over a page. 'And I did lots of other things, like riding on a reindeer sledge and a snowmobile.'

'I can get a flight from Kiruna airport to Stockholm tomorrow morning,' his mum said, looking at her phone, 'then pick up a connecting flight to Manchester.'

'We should all go together,' Hal said, and Uncle Nat nodded.

'Can you get us all tickets?' Uncle Nat asked. 'I'll tell James that I'll be home a day later than expected. Perhaps I can do a spot of Christmas shopping in Manchester. I didn't get as much done on this trip as I thought I would.'

Hal's mum laughed. 'I can't think why!'

There was a knock at the cabin door and they all turned.

'Nathaniel?' came a familiar voice, and the door opened. Standing on the snowy doorstep was Mortimer, flanked by serious-looking men in dark suits. 'Oh, Nathaniel! Harrison!' Morti exclaimed, hurrying in. She looked at Hal's mum. 'Beverly? Is that you? I haven't seen you for years! What are you doing here?'

'It's a long story. It's good to see you, Morti.'

'The Kill Code,' Morti exclaimed, looking at Uncle Nat. 'It's inside my wedding ring!'

'Yes.' Uncle Nat nodded.

'It's gone,' Hal said. 'We destroyed it.'

Mortimer dropped into an armchair and put her head in her hands and for a second Hal thought she was upset. 'Thank goodness,' she moaned. 'I've been so worried.'

'What happened at the hotel?' Uncle Nat asked her. 'Where did you disappear to?'

'The Swedish Intelligence Services were waiting in my room for me, after we said goodnight in the bar.' She nodded at the two men who were standing either side of the cabin door. 'They told me I was in danger. That I was the target of an assassin called the Chameleon who'd been hired by Björn. I could barely believe it, but they insisted I went with them to a safe house straight away. I only had time to leave the cabin keys for you, Nathaniel.' She bit her lip. 'I would never have given them to you if I had known what was on that ring. After the avalanche, when that man that she shot was taken into hospital, the Intelligence Service spoke with him.' She looked at Hal. 'He told them about the wedding ring and said that you'd gone after it.'

'You couldn't bring yourself to throw away your wedding ring, could you?' Hal said. 'You wore it on a necklace for a while, but then, when you won the Nobel Prize, you moved it to your key fob.'

'I was sentimental.' Morti shook her head. 'When we were married, Björn told me that he'd had a star named after

224

me . . . that the numbers on the inside of the ring were the coordinates of its position in the firmament – another one of his lies. I didn't know those numbers were the Kill Code. I realize now, I was foolish. I should have known Björn has never been romantic like that.'

'But why did he put it inside the ring?' Hal wondered.

'You know in the marriage vows, where you say, "*Till death do us part*"?' Morti replied. 'When he put that ring on my finger, he probably thought it was funny. He believed that the death sound, the Kill Code, would bind us together – a discovery that would make us rich beyond our wildest dreams. I believe he was planning to tell me about it, but I worked it out first.'

'Well, it's over now,' Uncle Nat said.

'How did you destroy the ring?' Morti asked Hal.

'I melted it in the furnace at the iron-ore mine,' Hal said, holding up a picture he'd drawn the previous night of the furnace.

'It's really gone?' Mortimer was so relieved that tears welled up in her eyes. 'The thought that I may have helped create a terrible weapon simply because I was too sentimental to throw away my wedding ring has been torturing me. I hate the thought that Björn knew I wouldn't get rid of it.'

'Well, you don't need to worry about the Chameleon any more,' Hal said. 'Mum took her out. No problem.'

Morti looked at Hal's mum with surprise and blinked.

'What about the Shadow?' Uncle Nat asked one of the Intelligence officers. 'Will he recover from his injuries?'

'Yes. He is held in a secure hospital facility,' the agent
replied. 'He will face trial when he has recovered.'

Uncle Nat replied with a wry smile and said, 'We'll see.'

After a hearty brunch, over which they told Mortimer the
whole story of their adventure on the night train to Narvik,
they bundled themselves into a taxi, which drove them along
dark, snowy roads between fir trees, before coming to a halt
outside a cluster of pretty wooden cabins in a clearing beside
the quiet road.

Lanterns blazed and festoon lamps were hung between

wooden poles and stalls. The air smelled of mulled wine, and cinnamon.

'Lars!' Uncle Nat waved at the architect, who was eating a piece of gingerbread by a stall selling reindeer pelts. 'Have you recovered from yesterday's avalanche?'

'Just about.' The man greeted them with a warm smile. 'I was heading into the ice building – the procession is about to start.'

Hal and the others followed the architect to a sprawling hangar made entirely of ice. Its walls were curved, like an igloo, the carved white bricks looking as steady and solid as concrete. As they entered the main hall, Hal marvelled at a display of glistening translucent sculptures set on plinths, illuminated by lights in the frosty floor. They gathered at the sides of the hall. The Dynamic Dozen were seated in a semi circle in the corner, with their instruments. Magnus lifted his baton and immediately they all focused intently on him. They began to play a hauntingly beautiful melody.

Taking a bite from his cinnamon bun, Hal watched with interest as the procession started. A girl with long wavy blonde hair, wearing a crown of electric candles on her head and dressed in white, processed into the hall as the lights dimmed. She represented Lucia, a mythical figure who brings light to the dark Swedish winters. Following her were boys carrying sticks with stars on the end, and girls carrying candles. The girls were Lucia's handmaidens. Hal spotted Katarina and wanted to wave, but she looked very serious and seemed to be concentrating hard on her singing. Behind them came a troupe of little children dressed in red costumes that reminded Hal of the troll that he'd got his little sister Ellie.

The girl who was Lucia stopped and sang a song that reminded Hal of Christmas carols, and all the other children joined in. Hal's mum, who loved carols, got tearful and put her arm around him.

When they finished their song, the Dynamic Dozen played

a festive tune. Then the orchestra and the choir of children joined together, making the ice hall reverberate with music.

Hal thought the whole thing was magical, and longed to be at home with Dad, Ellie and Bailey the dog, getting ready for Christmas.

After the procession was over, Hal found Katarina. 'I

wanted to wave to you,' Hal said, handing over a bag that contained her gákti, 'but you looked so serious.'

Katarina snorted. 'I was trying not to laugh at the size of the cinnamon bun you had stuffed in your mouth.'

As a leaving gift, Hal gave Katarina a portrait he'd drawn of her and Girjak the reindeer. 'I put my address on the back, you know, in case you ever want to visit England.'

'I have my reindeer herd to look after,' she said, 'but maybe one day. This picture is wonderful. Thank you. It was interesting to have an adventure with you, but I am happy that it is over now.'

'I know what you mean.' Hal nodded. 'Sometimes adventures on trains are the best thing in the world, but sometimes it's even better to be with friends and family, and for life to be calm and normal.'

'I heard that!' Hal's mum said happily, coming up behind them. 'How about our next holiday is spent lying by a pool, in the hot sunshine? If you want a crime to solve, you can read a good murder mystery book.'

'Deal,' Hal said with a grin.

A NOTE FROM
THE AUTHORS

Dear Reader,

The railway journey at the heart of this story is real, and we were lucky enough to travel it for ourselves while researching this book in November 2021. We have tinkered with the truth in a few places to help the engine of our adventure run more smoothly, but for the most part, if you take the night train to Narvik – and we recommend that you do – you will recognize the world in which our fiction takes place.

Kungsträdgården Station

The deepest station on Stockholm's metro is truly a cave of wonders, exactly as we depicted it in this story. It's home to colourful paintings, hidden relics, two unique species of fungi, its own self-sustaining ecosystem, and a breed of spider found nowhere else in Scandinavia: scientists aren't sure how it got there. Kungsträdgården Station is one of many brilliant and colourful examples of art and engineering on the Stockholm metro.

The Night Train to Narvik

Anyone can follow Hal and Uncle Nat's journey to the Arctic. The sleeper train to Narvik, calling at Kiruna, leaves Stockholm Central Station all year round. We have been as faithful as possible in our descriptions of the locomotive, carriages and compartments. Sam even tried reindeer stew in the dining car. (It was delicious!)

The Ofoten Line

The stretch of railway between Kiruna and Narvik is one of the most beautiful in the world. It makes an impressive journey through a treacherous mountain range between Norway and Sweden, traversing giant fjords with breathtaking views.

It carries passenger trains, but its main purpose is to link the iron-ore mine at Kiruna, in Sweden, with the port of Narvik, on the Norwegian coast. Sweden has its own ports, but they freeze over in winter. Even though it is further north, warm water currents from the Atlantic keep Narvik's port open all year round – making the journey through the mountains necessary.

The freight trains which appear in this story are based on the real IORE locomotives that carry their cargo to the coast. With iron-ore loads of up to 8,600 tonnes, these are some of the heaviest trains in the world.

The Sinking Town

Kiruna really is sinking! The enormous mine has made the ground around the old town unstable, and the residents are moving to a new town built about five kilometres to the east. But many buildings are coming with them. About 3,000 structures, including churches and houses, are being picked up and moved from the old town. Sometimes this is done brick by brick, and sometimes the whole building is put on the back of a truck and driven to the new town. Kiruna will finish relocating in 2035 – this slow 'crawling' has given Kiruna the nickname of 'the millipede town'.

Avalanches and Accidents

It is extremely unlikely that an avalanche would derail a train on the stretch of track before Kiruna. This is partly because there just aren't steep enough hills or mountains there, but also because the Swedish railway companies take great care to protect their lines from damage by snow. Between Kiruna and Narvik, the line passes through great 'snow sheds' in the mountains, protecting the railway tracks from sudden snowfall. Many locomotives are equipped with snowploughs to keep the lines clear, and special snow-clearing trains are used to remove heavy snowfall from tracks.

However, shortly before we visited Sweden, there was a freight train derailment on the line near Kiruna, and as we travelled along the tracks there, we saw the empty cargo trucks at the side of the line for ourselves. This helped inform our idea to have a train derailment in our story.

Modern railway accidents are rare, and trains are one of the safest ways to travel. Derailments do happen from time to time, but most of them don't cause any injuries to passengers.

Cleverly designed trains and hi-tech signalling mean that train travel is getting even safer every year.

Reindeer and the Sámi

The Sámi are the indigenous people of northern Norway, Sweden, Finland and Russia: an area known as Sápmi. This area used to be known by some people as Lapland, but this term is found offensive by the Sámi, who prefer it to be called by the name in their own language.

The Sámi people have lived in the Arctic for thousands of years, and are famous for herding reindeer. Traditionally, they would use the reindeer to pull sleds, eat their meat for food, use their hides for clothes, and their antlers for tools. Groups of Sámi families would live and work together to manage a herd of reindeer, travelling together with the animals as they migrated through the year. The Sámi divide the year into eight seasons, based on the migration habits of the herd.

About 10 per cent of all the Sámi people are involved in reindeer herding today. There is even a special reindeer school in Norway where young Sámi people can learn how to look after the animals.

The Magic Frequency and the Kill Code

Ultrasound really has been used to treat cancer. Focused sound waves have been found to break down some cancer cells while leaving normal cells in the body unharmed, though it is not a perfect treatment and it is not suitable for every patient. Morti's discovery, we imagined, would be a collection of frequencies that would make sound treatment more effective for more people. Many doctors think this is possible – we just haven't discovered it yet.

Thankfully, there is no Kill Code – no sound which can kill a person. But sound has often been used as a weapon in other ways. Highly powerful sound waves can damage people's eardrums, or make them feel sick. 'Sound cannons' have sometimes been used to disperse crowds, and very high-pitched sounds, which can only be heard by young people, have sometimes been used in public places to discourage teenagers from lingering there.

The Ice Hotel

The Ice Hotel is real, and we were lucky enough to visit it on our journey through Kiruna. Each winter, a new hotel is built from ice and snow, sculpted by designers and architects from all over the world, who each take on a different room. All the furniture is made from ice – even the beds! But visitors can sleep on reindeer hides wrapped in polar sleeping bags to keep them warm. Or, like Hal (and us!), they can choose to sleep in warm wooden cabins, admiring the hotel as a work of art.

The Northern Lights

The Northern Lights, also called the Aurora Borealis, are caused by the collision of tiny particles from space with the Earth's atmosphere, drawn to the North Pole by the Earth's magnetic field. The same effect can be seen at the South Pole: there it's called the Aurora Australis.

Sadly, we never got to see the Northern Lights on our visit to the Arctic. But that just gives us the perfect reason to travel back there again some day.

Find Out More . . .

If you'd like to learn more about the railways of the world, Sam has written a fantastic non-fiction book called *Epic Adventures*, exploring the world through twelve of his favourite train journeys. It includes many journeys from the Adventures on Trains series, including the sleeper train from Stockholm to Narvik, The Ghan in Australia, and the California Zephyr. It's beautifully illustrated by Sam Brewster, and combines incredible maps with amazing facts.

Visit **adventuresontrains.com** to learn about Hal's other adventures, for videos, classroom resources, drawing and other activities.

ACKNOWLEDGEMENTS

Bringing this series to readers has been a labour of love for a number of people at Macmillan Children's Books, and we would like to express our deepest gratitude to them all.

First and foremost, we would like to thank our editor, Sarah Hughes, who rides on the footplate of Team Steam and makes sure our trains arrive on schedule and in one piece. She works tirelessly to make these books what they are, and we are grateful to her for doing so. Thank you, Sarah.

A big thank you to Jo Hardacre, for telling the world about these books, and making sure we don't get up to too much mischief on the road. Thank you to Sarah Plows, whose innovative marketing has brought these adventures to the attention of new readers.

We owe a debt of gratitude to the peerless Rachel Vale, who expertly weaves the many moving parts of these books' design together, a job which seems like doing a jigsaw in a hurricane.

There have been so many people who've worked on the

series to whom we wish to say thank you: Venetia Gosling was the editor who brought this series to Macmillan and marshalled this book to the printers, Lucy Pearse edited the first three stories, Kat McKenna and Ella Chapman flew the flags for the first two books, Antonia Wilkinson tooted the whistle, and Nick de Somogyi has been our terrific copy-editor.

Thank you of course to Sam, Charlie, Amy, Emily, Louisa, Alyx, Belinda, and everyone else at Macmillan who has worked on these books in a variety of ways and helped make the series a success. We are tremendously grateful to all of you.

We would like to thank Kirsty McLachlan, our stellar agent; the wonderful Jot Davies, who we enjoy tormenting with terribly specific accents but who has never let us down, and Sam Harmsworth-Sparling, who is only married to one of us but takes such brilliant care of us both.

Our thanks to the incredible booksellers, librarians, teachers and parents who have done tireless work to champion Hal's adventures. We will always be grateful for everything you've done to help put our stories in the hands of readers.

But the last word must go to our indefatigable illustrator Elisa Paganelli, the eyes and hands of Hal himself. She has travelled with us through six incredible adventures, adjusting her art style to each, and created over *two hundred and fifty* beautiful and painstakingly specific illustrations, wrapped in six beautiful covers, which have brough us such joy and delight. She is also the nicest human being imaginable. Thank you, Elisa. You're amazing. It's been a pleasure to have you aboard.

Sam Sedgman

My parents have always given me a tremendous amount of love and support, and I would not be the writer I am today without them. Thank you for always being such tremendous champions of my work, of this series in particular, and for the brilliant childhood adventures which have inspired so much of it. Thanks also to my two brilliant nephews, Monty and Sully. I hope we get to have our own adventures one day.

I have had tremendous support this year from many friends old and new, who have filled my life with colour and joy. You are too numerous to mention, but my special thanks must go to Bob, Kim and Roisin, and to Ben Hallett for helping equip me for my Arctic expedition.

Thank you as well to all my author buddies who make this job a lot less lonely, and a lot more fun. Especially to my band of merry men: Andy, Ben and Rich. Thank you for the gay ol' times.

And lastly, to Maya, my delightful co-author, who for the past five years has been a tireless source of inspiration, a fantastic companion for adventure, and an irreplaceable friend. I will be forever grateful to you for all you have helped me achieve. Thank you.

M. G. Leonard

Huge thanks to my partner in creating crimes, Sam Sedgman, for igniting a passion within me for train travel. What a ride we've had! I've loved every adventure and learned so much writing this series. Thanks Pal.

This series of stories wouldn't exist without the loving support and encouragement from my family: Sam Harmsworth-Sparling, Arthur and Sebastian. My boys inspired the idea for the series and I'm truly grateful for the journey it's taken me on. I would like to say thank you to Clare Rakich who has listened to my concerns, grumbles and read all of these books. And a special acknowledgement goes to Holly Smale and Maz Evans who keep me sane. Kirsty McLachlan, you know that you're my hero, the wind beneath my wings.

Join Hal and Uncle Nat right from the start of their

ADVENTURES ON TRAINS

'A thrilling and entertaining adventure story'
David Walliams on
The Highland Falcon Thief

'A first-class choo-choo dunnit!'
David Solomons on
Kidnap on the California Comet

'A high-speed train journey worth catching . . . The best yet'
The Times on
Murder on the Safari Star

'A super-fun middle-grade mystery' Peter Bunzl, author of *Cogheart*

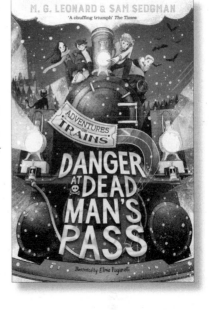

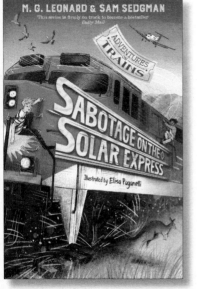

'Like Murder on the Orient Express but better. A terrific read!'
Frank Cottrell-Boyce

ABOUT THE
AUTHORS

M. G. Leonard has made up stories since she was a girl, but back then adults called them lies or tall tales and she didn't write them down. As a grown up, her favourite things to create stories about are beetles, birds and trains. Her books have been translated into over forty languages and won many awards. She is the vice president of the insect charity Buglife, and a founding author of Authors4Oceans. She lives in Brighton with her husband, two sons, a fat cat called Kasper, a dog called Nell, and a variety of exotic beetles.

Sam Sedgman is a bestselling author, presenter, and keen ferroequinologist. A lifelong fan of crime fiction, he used to make murder mystery treasure hunts for a living, and still makes his family play Cluedo at Christmas. He grew up with a railway line at the bottom of his garden and has been mad about trains ever since. He lives in London.

Elisa Paganelli was born in Italy and since childhood hasn't been able to resist the smell of paper and pencils. She graduated from the European Institute of Design in Turin and worked in advertising, as well as running an award-winning design shop and studio. She now collaborates as a freelance designer with publishers and advertising agencies all over the world, including designing and illustrating *The House With Chicken Legs* (Usborne) and the Travels of Ermine series (Usborne).